RUN GIRL

EVA HUDSON

– VENATRIX –

RUN GIRL

EVA HUDSON

First published 2014 by Two Pies Press
This edition published 2015 by Venatrix

ISBN: 978-0-9932679-0-1

RUN GIRL

For the fans: your support has meant so much

ONE

Sitting in a luxury State Department limousine, Jayne Whitticker stared out across the wide runway toward the specially adapted Boeing 757. Through the tinted windows of the car the dark skies glowering over Andrew's Air Force Base seemed even more oppressive than they had when she'd arrived ten minutes ago. A shiver ran across her shoulders. The clouds, heavy with snow, promised a blizzard later that day. Secretary of State Whitticker would be halfway across the Atlantic by then. She couldn't help but wonder whether the threatening storm was some sort of omen for what lay ahead.

In the distance, the faint wail of a siren started up. Whitticker leaned forward in her seat. Automatically, the thick glass partition separating the front seats from the back buzzed down.

"Is that something we need to be concerned about, James?"

The man in the black suit murmured something into a discreet microphone clipped to the sleeve of his jacket, then waited. "Minor security breach on the other side of the base, ma'am. Nothing for you to worry about."

"Thank you."

"Ma'am?" His voice was hesitant, unsure.

"Yes?"

"We should really be boarding now. The weather is deteriorating."

"Give me a few more moments, James."

The partition buzzed back up again.

Jayne Whitticker looked up at the snowy sky. She was about to face the biggest task of her career. The biggest she was ever likely to take on. At sixty-four, she knew her position as Secretary of State would probably be the last professional role she'd hold. She'd only had the job a few weeks, following the premature retirement of her predecessor. Before his heart condition had forced him to step down, he had been conducting difficult negotiations between three warring African nations, in an attempt to broker a peace deal and halt the slaughter of innocent civilians. It was a mission she had now inherited. In just over seven hours she would be sitting in a room in Strasbourg with the leaders of those three nations and their many aides. The eyes of the world would be on her.

The partition buzzed back down again. She should really be getting on that plane. She took a deep breath and straightened her spine. This might be the toughest job of her career, but it was also the most prestigious. She had an opportunity to help make an enormous change for the better. That was a task to be relished, not feared. "All right, James, I'm ready."

"Actually, ma'am, we can't move right now."

"James?"

"The security breach is more serious than we first thought."

"I have to get on that plane."

"You will, ma'am. Have no doubt about that."

"What exactly is happening?"

"An individual was causing a disturbance at the entrance nearest the access road. The guard on duty raised the alert level accordingly."

"What kind of disturbance?"

Before her chief security advisor could answer, Jayne Whitticker saw a black SUV swerve to a stop right next to her limousine. "James?"

"It's all right ma'am. The individual is known to us. There's no further threat."

The partition moved back up again.

Outside, a special agent yanked open the rear passenger door of the SUV and, wearing a thin hooded coat and skinny jeans, the Secretary of State's granddaughter, Rachel, jumped out. She had a small backpack slung across one shoulder and a coy expression on her face. The agent opened the door of the State Department limousine and Rachel climbed inside. She was shivering.

"How did you get here?" Jayne Whitticker held the eighteen year old's ungloved hands in hers. "You're frozen to the bone."

Rachel sniffed then wiped a sleeve across her nose. "I hitched."

"For God's sake, what have I told you about that?"

"I know for a fact you hitched right across the country in the sixties and seventies. If it was OK for you then it's—"

"Times are different now, more dangerous."

"I had to come see you before you left."

"Do your mother and father know you're here?"

Rachel Whitticker wriggled her shoulders and turned away.

"You've had another fight?"

"Biggest one yet."

"What was it about this time?"

"Dad wants me to go to college to study Math. I want to go to acting class. He won't even listen to what I have to say."

The things teenagers consider important, Jayne Whitticker thought. "How about majoring in Math? You could still take classes in theater and drama."

The partition buzzed down again. "Madam Secretary? We really do have to board the plane now," James said.

Rachel ignored him. "I even suggested that. I told you—he won't listen. He's being a bully."

A strong stubborn streak ran through Whitticker's family: everyone determined to hold their ground until the argument wasn't so much won or lost, but rendered irrelevant.

"I'll be right there, James."

Jayne Whitticker had recognized long ago that she always took her favorite grandchild's side over her son's. It had become her default position. "A big fight doesn't explain your presence here." She squeezed Rachel's hand. "You know what this trip is for. You know what I'm going to Europe to try to achieve. How important it is."

"And you know I wouldn't be here if there were any way I could stay with them without imploding."

"Oh come on, Rachel. Are you seriously suggesting you come with me?" Jayne Whitticker pulled her hand away and studied her granddaughter's face closely.

"If I come with you it'd give mom and dad a chance to calm down some. Maybe see things from a different perspective. Especially if you spoke to dad."

The Secretary of State shook her head. "I can't take you with me. I can't. It's just not possible."

"Ma'am, I really have to insist now. The weather is closing in."

"You wouldn't even notice me. I promise I'll behave myself."

James climbed out of the car and grabbed the handle of the rear passenger door.

"Please, Grams." She pulled a pained expression. "I don't know what might happen if I stay."

"You can't get your own way through emotional blackmail. Please credit me with enough sense to see through that ploy."

"I know how smart you are. And I'm so proud of you. What you're about to do."

"Flattery doesn't cut it either." Jayne Whitticker glanced down at Rachel's left wrist, at the scar running from the base of her palm three inches up her arm. This wasn't the first time her granddaughter had spoken about imploding. Rachel needed her support right now. The timing couldn't have been worse. "I take it you remembered to bring your passport?"

Rachel dug a hand into her backpack and retrieved the dark blue rectangular booklet.

"You'll have to have a chaperone once we're over there. A private security guard. You do know I won't be able to spend any time with you?"

"I understand. I told you—I'll totally behave myself. I won't embarrass you."

The door opened next to the Secretary of State. James' black jacket flapped in the strong wind. A few moments later Jayne and Rachel Whitticker were helped from the car to the steps of the waiting plane.

When Jayne Whitticker was buckled into her seat for take off, she took a moment to wonder at the wisdom of her decision, but before she had time to change her mind, her cell phone started to ring. She knew without looking who was calling. She answered quickly and listened carefully to an intense sixty second pep talk.

"Don't worry, Mr President," she said when it was her turn to speak. "The negotiations are in safe hands. I won't let you down."

TWO

The line for refreshments was moving slowly. Special Agent Ingrid Skyberg shuffled along patiently even though she was well aware the dark brown liquid that emerged from the plastic flask at the head of the table would taste nothing like coffee, or have any of its restorative effects.

A female detective joined the end of the line. Ingrid remembered her asking a raft of engaged and intelligent questions the day before. "Morning," the woman said.

Ingrid turned to face her. "Good morning. I'm sorry—I didn't catch your name yesterday."

The detective shoved out a hand. "Detective Inspector Natasha McKittrick."

They shook hands. "Pleased to meet you."

"I just wanted to let you know I got a lot out of yesterday's sessions. Child protection isn't a specialism of mine, but I do like to keep up on the latest investigation techniques." The line shuffled forward again. "I'm sorry I can't say the same for some of my colleagues."

Ingrid didn't want to speak out of turn, but she had found the lack of engagement in the previous day's training sessions surprising. "Were some of them recruited onto the course… involuntarily?"

"Oh no—they all signed up of their own free will. It's an excuse to get out of the station, get a free lunch and take it easy for a couple of days. No reflection on you or your colleagues. Or the FBI in general."

"Do you have any tips? Anything we can do to shake things up a little?"

"Do something unexpected. Something that might at least keep them awake until lunchtime."

"Any idea what that might be?"

"You're on your own there."

Finally Ingrid reached the flask labeled 'coffee' and pumped out a small cup of dark liquid. "My coffee shop espresso seems an awful long while ago now."

"This stuff is pretty foul, isn't it?" The detective smiled at her. "Anyway—I just wanted to let you know you're not totally wasting your time—some of us are getting a lot out of this." With that DI McKittrick grabbed herself a tea and nodded a goodbye to Ingrid. Ingrid watched her settle into a seat right at the back of the overheated conference room.

Ingrid took her coffee to the front of the room and sat down behind a narrow wooden table, waiting for her two colleagues from the FBI's Violent Crimes Against Children program to arrive. As she watched the rows of seats slowly fill, she wondered at the unexpected and slightly bizarre nature of the situation. Forty-eight hours ago she'd had no clue she'd be sitting in a stuffy subterranean conference room in New Scotland Yard. When one of the regular trainers had been forced to pull out because his wife had gone into premature labor, Ingrid's boss had asked her to step in at the last minute. She'd said yes without hesitation: not only did she relish the prospect of helping out a colleague in need, but doing a little sightseeing in London just a couple of weeks before Christmas really couldn't be turned down. But so far all she'd seen was the inside of a hotel room in Marylebone, this conference room in New Scotland Yard and the interior of a black London taxi cab.

A few minutes later her colleagues arrived and shortly after that the morning training session began. Thirty minutes into the session a noisy cell phone ringtone sounded from the center of the room. A middle-aged cop struggled to his feet, waved his phone in the air, and said, "Really sorry, everyone, but I can't ignore this. Boss would kill me." He flashed an inauthentic smile and swiftly headed toward the exit.

Ingrid glanced at her two Bureau colleagues. Kevin Price shrugged back at her. Lucille Gardiner, who was standing at the lectern, merely scowled a little harder than she had been prior to the interruption.

The cop was their first bailout of the morning. Ingrid suspected he wouldn't be the last. She scrutinized the remaining detectives and tried to guess which ones wouldn't make it to the end of the course the following day. She noticed that one bald guy at the back, carrying forty or so extra pounds, was actually asleep. Any minute now she was sure he'd start snoring. Just like yesterday, none of the audience seemed particularly interested. Ingrid wondered what unexpected event she could manufacture that might shake them up. Nothing obvious sprang to mind.

Despite the overall lack of interest from the crowd, Lucille continued with her Powerpoint presentation as if her audience were hanging on her every word. Ingrid could only admire her dogged determination. Five riveting multi-media slides later, Lucille's cell phone started to vibrate noisily against the aluminum lectern. Ingrid's colleague grabbed the glasses hanging on the chain around her neck and read the text message. As she read each word, her eyes widened incrementally. By the time she was done her mouth had fallen open. "I'm so sorry about this, folks—but I have to leave. I'm sure Agents Skyberg and Price will manage in my absence." She grabbed her jacket and purse and hurried toward the door.

Kevin and Ingrid exchanged bemused glances. Lucille *hated* cell phone interruptions—in training programs, meetings, or any other place she reasonably expected the participants' undivided attention. Ingrid worried one of Lucille's kids might be sick. She thought about running after her, just to see if there was anything she could do, but as she started to get up, the expression on Kevin Price's face begged her to stay exactly where she was. She watched the door swing shut behind Lucille. The event was certainly unexpected, but Ingrid wasn't sure it was quite what DI McKittrick had had in mind when she'd made her suggestion.

"So! Where were we?" Kevin jumped from his seat and took up Lucille's place at the lectern. He gestured toward the Powerpoint slide displayed on the large white screen behind him.

Kevin Price was a true professional. All Ingrid's colleagues working in the Violent Crimes Against Children program were. Pretty much every single one of them felt they were on a mission. But there was so much to do. No matter how hard they worked, or how many agents were assigned to the program at any one time, it always felt a little like chipping away at an iceberg with a toothpick. After three years working in the program, Ingrid had started to wonder if she'd made much of a difference at all.

From her very first day at the Academy in Quantico, Ingrid had always wanted to work in child protection. Through all her years at far flung field offices, she had been focused on that single goal. All along, in the back of her mind, she'd had some fantastical notion that she'd stumble on a pedophile ring that would somehow lead her to her missing school friend, Megan. She'd harbored a wild hope that she would discover some isolated derelict house where her best friend had been held for the last eighteen years. That she'd be able to rescue her and finally make amends.

And maybe get a little peace of mind.

But Megan was probably dead, in all likelihood killed shortly after her abduction. Although the unfavorable statistics hadn't stopped Ingrid searching, as each year passed and she'd chased down yet another false lead, her hope had been pretty much extinguished. Maybe it was time for a change. Time to get out of the program. Perhaps she could use this trip away from home, from her normal work environment, to give herself a little space to think, to decide what she should do next with her career.

At the lectern, Kevin's voice had gotten a little louder. Ingrid glanced up at her colleague then at the screen behind him. It displayed the last slide of the session.

"OK, people," Kevin said. "Fifteen minutes before we break for coffee. Let's try a little role play based on what we've just learned." Kevin's suggestion was met with a roomful of groans—the most vocal the audience had been. "Hey! Come on, just fifteen minutes. Then I've got a very special delivery arriving direct from Krispy Kreme."

At the back of the room, Ingrid noticed DI McKittrick smiling and shaking her head. Ingrid caught her eye and smiled back at her. A moment later Ingrid's phone started to vibrate in her pocket. She was careful to wait until Kevin was busy dividing the hostile audience into groups of three before she read the text message:

-URGENT-

car waiting for you outside leave immediately await further instructions

THREE

The black sedan with diplomatic plates was parked right outside the main entrance of New Scotland Yard. The driver, wearing a black suit, crisp white shirt and dark glasses, opened the rear passenger door for Ingrid. She climbed in to discover Lucille Gardiner inside.

"What's going on?" Ingrid asked her.

"I haven't a clue. This guy's not giving anything away." She gestured a hand toward the driver who had silently and quickly slipped behind the wheel.

He started the engine.

"What about my colleague?" Ingrid said, leaning forward. "Shouldn't we wait for him?"

The driver's voice piped into the back of the car via a small speaker embedded in the parcel shelf. "I have my instructions—collect Agents Gardiner and Skyberg from New Scotland Yard and return to the embassy."

"The embassy?" Ingrid had suspected the American embassy was their intended destination as soon as she noticed the diplomatic registration plates. "Who gave you those instructions?"

"I can't tell you that."

The driver glanced over his shoulder at Ingrid then turned eyes front and pulled away from the curb without saying another word.

Ingrid settled back into the plush upholstery of the luxurious sedan. She supposed she might as well enjoy the journey. After a few moments she turned to Lucille. "What did your text say?" Her colleague showed her the screen of her cell phone. "Same as mine," Ingrid told her. "Strange they weren't both sent at the same time."

"Maybe they didn't want to raise any alarm."

"Should we, do you think? Be alarmed?"

Lucille shrugged. "Guess we'll find out soon enough. If it were a national emergency you'd think Kevin would have gotten the text too."

"I'm just glad it's nothing to do with your kids. I was a little worried back there."

"Thank God. But I should call them. I don't know when I'll next get the chance." Lucille turned toward the window and hit the speed dial option on her phone.

Ingrid stared through the glass on her side, watching the pedestrians on the sidewalk and studying the architecture lining the busy street. There was a lot of new construction happening on the northern side—

all glass and steel curves. On their side of the street she noticed a department store, a collection of retail outlets and fast food places that were familiar from back home and, as they approached a major intersection, set back from the road, a grand red brick cathedral, a tall bell tower standing on the left hand side. She craned her neck to get a better look. After another couple of intersections she saw a sign for Buckingham Palace—one of the places she planned to visit on Thursday before her flight home—but was disappointed that all she could see from the car was a long, dull brick wall, razor wire running along the top.

A few minutes later they were heading roughly north, a large expanse of green on their left hand side. Ingrid supposed this had to be Hyde Park. The embassy wasn't far from here. She'd done a little research during the plane ride over. She'd attempted to memorize the rough locations of all the important landmarks in central London: the embassy, New Scotland Yard, obviously, Thames House—the headquarters of MI5—and 'Babylon-on-Thames'—the headquarters of MI6. Not exactly regular tourist haunts.

Sure enough, after another five minutes, they were pulling into a dinky little street blocked at the end by a metal gate. Beyond that was a heavy duty yellow and white striped road blocker.

A few yards out, the gates opened and the road blocker descended. The driver was so well practiced, he barely needed to adjust his speed as he drove the car in.

Lucille finally said goodbye to her oldest daughter and hung up.

"Everything OK at home?" Ingrid asked her.

"Only the usual dramas—forgotten soccer strip, lost lunch money. Nothing Stuart can't handle."

Once inside the compound, the driver continued into an underground parking lot a couple of stories below ground level. He parked up and the speaker behind them crackled into life.

"This is your stop, agents." He swiveled in his seat and pulled off his sunglasses for the first time. "Have a pleasant visit."

Before Ingrid had a chance to open her door, it swung wide. An armed female guard was standing to attention as Ingrid climbed out. An identical guard performed the same task for Lucille on the other side of the car. Ingrid wasn't sure what to make of the VIP treatment. Was it a good or a bad sign? For a fleeting moment it almost felt as if they were under arrest. Ingrid had managed to escape one of the least rewarding training sessions she'd ever attended, but what exactly had she escaped to? She pictured Kevin Price manfully holding the fort at the Metropolitan Police's HQ and hoped he hadn't had to deal with rebellion in the ranks before the donuts arrived.

Across the parking lot an elevator opened and a middle-aged man with gray speckled dark curly hair stepped out. He was wearing an unflattering pair of corduroy pants and a check shirt. He reminded Ingrid of her high school geography teacher. The man peered around the parking lot, spotted the car and strode toward them. His face broke into a grin.

"Special Agent Gardiner!" he said and extended his hand as he hurried to Lucille's side of the car.

Ingrid wondered if the two had met before. From the bemused look on Lucille's face, she supposed not.

"And by a process of elimination I guess you must be Special Agent Skyberg." He grabbed one of Lucille's elbows and steered her around the car. Then he shook hands with Ingrid. "So… I'm thinking you probably both have a lot of questions for me, huh?"

FOUR

Ingrid returned Sol Franklin's smile and nodded. She had so many questions that she said nothing at all: she didn't want to risk bombarding the man with them all at once. She glanced at Lucille, who, uncharacteristically, seemed equally dumbstruck.

"Where are my manners?" he said. "I am the assistant deputy chief of the Bureau's Legal Attaché program here at the embassy. Sol Franklin, at your service." He gave a little bow. "Actually, I'm rather hoping you'll both be at the program's service for the next little while." He looked from Lucille back to Ingrid. "We have a..." He lowered his voice. "A *situation.*" He turned to the uniformed guards in turn and thanked them.

Ingrid had never known a superior officer be this courteous. Immediately she was suspicious—why was he being so goddamn nice? They followed him as he strode purposefully back to the elevator.

"First we need to get your embassy credentials processed," he told them as the elevator doors closed. "Should only take a couple minutes."

They traveled two floors up and were soon trailing behind him down a long wood paneled corridor. Lucille grabbed Ingrid's arm. She shook her head and shrugged. Ingrid shrugged back. What the hell was going on?

After another sixty feet of featureless wooden corridor, the space opened out onto a large reception area. On the far side a woman with wild frizzy hair was gesticulating extravagantly at a grave-faced, but completely emotionless Marine.

"Well, check again!" the woman hollered. "My editor arranged this for me herself. I thought you were meant to be organized." She glanced in Ingrid's direction. "And what are you gawping at? Have you never seen a member of the press asserting her rights?"

Ingrid looked at Sol, who was frowning at the woman.

"I suppose the notion of rights must be a bit of a novelty for you."

"Is there a problem, ma'am?" Sol's frown swiftly turned into a smile and he strode toward the desk.

"I'm supposed to have press accreditation for the upcoming visit. It was all arranged in advance. Somebody has ballsed it up."

"I'm so sorry to hear that, ma'am. If you wouldn't mind taking a seat for just a few moments, I'm sure we can remedy the situation."

Reluctantly, the woman in the flimsy raincoat and black patent leather boots sank onto one of the hard seats lining the wall. Sol mumbled something into his cell phone. The Marine was replaced by an identical one—save for the color of his hair—almost immediately. The original Marine sat at a nearby desk and, with Sol Franklin peering over his shoulder at the computer screen, got busy with his keyboard. Just a couple of minutes later, Sol returned to Ingrid and Lucille with freshly printed security passes hanging from US embassy branded lanyards. He started to lead them back toward the long corridor.

"Queuing is just a quaint old English tradition is it?" the woman in the raincoat called after them, as she jumped from her seat.

Ingrid marched toward her, her face fixed in as genuine a smile as she could manage. "I'm so sorry, ma'am. Back home I wouldn't dream of line jumping. It was very rude of us. Please forgive me." She smiled again, hoping she could disarm the woman with old fashioned Minnesota charm.

It didn't work.

"Good God, you're so fake, the lot of you! Do I look stupid? You'll have to try a bloody sight harder than that to make amends."

The replacement Marine cleared his throat behind them. "Miss Tate?" he said. "Your press pass is now approved—thank you for your patience."

'Miss Tate' hadn't taken her eyes off Ingrid. She raised a delicately plucked eyebrow at her. "Now that's the sort of sickly smarm I can deal with—at least I get what I want at the end of it." With that, she snapped her head toward the Marine and forced a smile.

Ingrid let out a breath. She practically felt as if she'd been assaulted by the angry reporter. The experience wasn't without its uses, however. It was the first Ingrid had heard about any upcoming 'visit'. She wondered how important the visitor to the embassy had to be, to generate such interest in the local press. Was it possible the president was planning a trip? Ingrid quickly dismissed the idea: how would an English reporter know about something like that ahead of FBI agents? She looked at Sol Franklin, who was standing with Lucille, waiting for her to join them in the corridor. So far he'd succeeded in revealing absolutely nothing.

They took the elevator to the fifth floor and Franklin led them down another wood paneled corridor to a room at the far end. He opened the door and stood to one side. There were two leather couches in the room, one along the wall facing the door and the other at right angles to it. In front of the couches stood a low table. A half dozen bottles of mineral water sat in the center. Apart from the three items of furniture and the water, the room was completely empty.

"Make yourselves comfortable," the assistant deputy chief told them and smiled. "I hope you understand—it's standard procedure in the circumstances—I need you to give me your cell phones."

Ingrid and Lucille exchanged glances.

"And tablets, etcetera, etcetera… anything electronic. We do have to insist on a communications lockdown, I'm afraid."

They handed over their cells and iPads. Ingrid was surprised to discover Lucille had somehow managed to squeeze two tablets and three cell phones into her purse.

Sol Franklin gathered the gadgets up and held them in his arms close to his chest, looking as if he'd just raided a branch of RadioShack. "I'll be right back." He turned toward the door, but was unable to open it.

Ingrid jumped up and levered down the handle for him. She opened the door to discover yet another Marine standing to attention outside. Sol gave Ingrid a curt nod and passed through the doorway. The guard pulled the door shut.

Then locked it.

FIVE

Lucille Gardiner jumped up from her seat and ran to the door. She rattled the handle. "Hey, what's going on out there!" She rattled it some more. "I think you've made a mistake."

A mumbled voice responded from outside. "Step away from the door, ma'am."

"What?"

Ingrid gestured for Lucille to move further into the room.

The lock clicked and the door slowly opened. The Marine looked at both of them in turn. "Anything I can help you with?"

"I don't appreciate being locked in here."

"It's protocol, ma'am." He started to close the door. "Nothing for you to worry about."

"Wait!" Lucille shouted.

"Ma'am?"

"How long are we going to be in here?"

"I don't have that information."

"Well can you go find that inform—" The door closed on her. "What the hell?" She looked at Ingrid, as if she might be able to explain.

"Franklin told us he'd be right back. Why don't we sit down, take a breather, huh?" Ingrid had never seen Lucille this twitchy before. But then she'd never seen her without a cell phone either.

"What if one of the girls needs to get in touch with me while we're locked away in here?"

"I'm sure we won't be here that long. Besides—you just checked in with them. Everything's fine back home."

"I'm sorry." She sank back down onto one of the couches. "I always promise them I'll be contactable whenever I'm away on these trips. It's the only way I can avoid tears and tantrums when the car arrives to take me to the airport."

Ingrid snapped the lid off a bottle of water and handed it to her colleague. "Let's give it ten minutes or so, shall we?" She grabbed a water for herself and sat down. She glanced around the room. There were no pictures or photographs decorating the walls, no rug to break up the dark surface of the wooden floor, and the ceiling was covered in foam tiles. The space certainly wasn't designed for comfort. Ingrid checked the corners of the ceiling and spotted a burglar alarm sensor attached to the corner nearest the door. Diagonally opposite was a sprinkler outlet. That had to be where the cameras were concealed. Ingrid assumed she and Lucille had been placed in the room for observation. Some kind of test ahead of an assignment. Why else would they have been abandoned like this? She tapped Lucille on the arm, made eye contact, then looked deliberately toward the sprinkler corner of the ceiling.

"What is it?" Lucille said, for some reason completely oblivious to Ingrid's cue.

"Nothing at all." Ingrid looked again toward the corner of the room, made eye contact again and tilted her head, willing Lucille to understand her this time.

"Are you feeling OK?"

Come on!

Ingrid slumped back onto the couch. "I'm perfectly fine. Just checking you're all right."

"I'd be better if I knew the door wasn't locked and there wasn't a six feet tall armed Marine on the other side of it."

"I'm sure the assistant deputy chief has important strategic work to do, while he assesses the situation. And the personnel involved." Again she glanced up toward the corner of the room.

"You would have figured he'd done that already. Otherwise why waste our time?"

It was hopeless. For some reason—maybe she was preoccupied worrying about her kids—Lucille's powers of perception had deserted her.

Lucille checked her watch. "Ten minutes and then I'm breaking down the door." She peered into her purse and pulled out a scrap of paper and a pen.

"What are you doing?"

"Making a list of all the questions for Franklin. Though I'm not sure this piece of paper is big enough."

Ingrid had plenty of questions herself. But a mental list would do just fine. As she sat there and absent-mindedly watched Lucille's pen scratch across the paper, Ingrid started to wonder why they'd chosen her and Lucille ahead of Kevin. He was just as experienced an agent. He had more years on the clock than Ingrid. Since the beginning of the trip he hadn't stopped mentioning the fact he was coming up to his tenth anniversary at the Bureau.

The only thing Ingrid and Lucille had in common was their gender. Ingrid was much more similar to Kevin than Lucille. Neither of them had kids, they both lived alone, they were both single. Ingrid blinked and opened her eyes wide. How could she have thought that about herself? She'd been engaged to Marshall for just under a year. *Unmarried.* That's what she'd meant. Both she and Kevin were unmarried. But they selected the two female agents—why? And why were they observing them like this? To see how they interacted? It seemed a little strange. What were they hoping to learn?

She settled back on the couch and took a long gulp of water. Then tried to tune out the mumbling of her colleague and attempted to trawl her mind for any scrap of information she'd ever learned about the FBI's mission overseas. The training course she'd been helping facilitate up until an hour ago was part of the program. Spreading Bureau best practice across the world was one of its aims. She knew that Sol Franklin had to be part of the Legal Attaché program. He'd be reporting to the chief of mission at the embassy. She also knew that more and more, the FBI's role within US embassies around the globe concerned counterterrorism and counterintelligence, with most of the Bureau's personnel dedicated to matters of national security.

But what could that have to do with her? Or Lucille? She wondered why the situation Sol Franklin had referred to couldn't be dealt with by any of their existing agents. Instead, they'd disrupted a training session to recruit agents from the Violent Crimes Against Children Program. Could the problem be related to a pedophile ring here in the UK? But why not include Kevin if that were the case?

Ingrid would have loved to discuss the issue with Lucille, but not with Sol Franklin potentially listening in. Instead, she decided it wise to keep her own counsel.

Fifteen minutes later Lucille was on her feet again, pacing the room. At the ten minute mark Ingrid had managed to persuade her that giving the assistant deputy chief another five minutes was a sensible thing to do. She doubted the same approach would work a second time. Just as Ingrid got to her feet, determined she should be the one to talk to the Marine stationed outside, the lock clicked and the door opened.

A grinning man in a smart gray suit and open-neck shirt stood in the doorway. A pair of Aviator sunglasses hung ostentatiously out of his breast pocket. Ingrid noticed his dark brown hair was cropped close to his scalp on either side of his head, with a flamboyant quiff of longer hair balanced on top. He was clean shaven, but his beard was already trying to push through his chin and cheeks. The man had a ten a.m. shadow. "Thank you so much for your patience, agents. I can only apologize for the wait." He had an English accent.

"Where's the assistant deputy chief?" Lucille barked at him.

"Sol's been unavoidably delayed, I'm afraid. He sent me in his stead." He smiled at Lucille then Ingrid, his gaze lingering a little longer on Ingrid's face than she was entirely comfortable with. "Agent Skyberg, would you mind coming with me?"

SIX

Ingrid tilted her head and frowned, but didn't make a move toward him.

Lucille stepped forward instead. "I'm not staying a minute longer in this goddamn cell." In two strides she was practically toe to toe with the English guy. "Are you getting out of my way voluntarily, or do I have to make you?"

Ingrid smiled to herself. Lucille was no more that five feet five, even in heels. But doubtless she could take on a six feet two British spook in a suit with no trouble at all.

"I have no intention of imprisoning you, Agent Gardiner." He smiled at her again, his teeth remarkably even and bright white. They almost sparkled in their perfection. Ingrid decided once he was through with MI6, he could audition for the next

James Bond movie. He stepped to one side to let Lucille into the corridor.

Ingrid followed her out. "What's happening?"

"All will be explained shortly."

"Why the mystery?"

"Oh—no mystery at all. Just a little disorganization, I'm afraid."

In the corridor they were confronted by another tall Marine. This one held all of Lucille's electronic equipment in a small transparent plastic bag.

"This charming young man will escort you to the car waiting in the basement," the Englishman told Lucille.

"What?"

"We're so sorry to have disrupted your day."

"We?"

"I'm speaking on behalf of the assistant deputy chief."

"That's it? You just want me to leave now?"

"Thank you so much for your time."

Lucille seemed almost disappointed to get her gadgets back and be released, even though she'd been talking about nothing else since they'd arrived. She could Skype her kids all day long now if she wanted. Ingrid tugged the plastic bag from the Marine's grasp and pushed it into Lucille's hands.

"Get out of here before he changes his mind."

Lucille looked blank-faced into the bag, then up at Ingrid. "I guess. But what about you?" She turned toward the British guy. "What are you planning to use Ingrid for?"

"I'm afraid I can't divulge sensitive information. I'm sure you understand." There was the bright white smile again. "Agent Skyberg? We should really be getting on." He nodded to Lucille, half-saluted the two Marines, and strode down the corridor. "If you'd like to follow me, agent?" he called over his shoulder.

Ingrid jogged to catch up with him.

A few minutes later they'd traveled two floors in the elevator, hurried down another wood-paneled corridor and were standing beside a tall rosewood door. The smartly dressed spook rapped on the door and pushed it open without waiting for a reply. He gestured for Ingrid to enter ahead of him.

Ingrid stepped into the room to discover Sol Franklin sitting behind a wide, untidy desk in front of a large window, the wooden-slatted shades pulled down. He was beaming at her. He stood up and pointed to a high-backed chair on the other side of his desk. "Nick's been looking after you, I hope?"

Ingrid turned to see the Englishman quietly closing the door. "I'm afraid *Nick* didn't get a chance to introduce himself."

"I can't believe my manners have been so lacking." The man strode toward her, his arm extended. He shook her hand. "Nicolas Angelis, Lead Advisor, Fortnum International Security, at your service."

Not a spook, then. At least not on the UK government payroll. Why was the US embassy using private security agents?

Angelis only released her hand after he'd given it a good firm squeeze. He winked at her. "My friends call me Nick." He walked to the left side of Sol Franklin's desk, folded his arms and leaned casually against a walnut file cabinet. One corner of his mouth twitched upward.

"I guess it's about time we told you why you're here." Sol Franklin opened a desk drawer and pulled out a cardboard file. He shoved away some of the clutter from the space immediately in front of him and carefully laid the file on the desk. He cleared his throat. His congested cough sounded as though he smoked two packs of cigarettes a day. "So… the situation we find ourselves in…" He steepled his fingers and pushed them under his chin. "Wait, let me start that again. The situation as it stands… Aw hell, there's no diplomatic way of saying this. We're in a goddamn crap hole. Somebody screwed up big time and it's up to us to pick up the pieces." He laid his stubby-fingered hands flat against the file.

Ingrid wondered who exactly he was referring to when using the word 'us'. The US? The embassy? The Bureau? And what the hell could it possibly have to do with her?

Sol Franklin cleared his throat again and said, "You may or may not be aware that the Secretary of State is in Strasbourg at the moment—that's in France, just in case your European geography is a little rusty—leading very delicate peace negotiations. It's taken a long time to get the various warring factions to even agree to set foot in the same country, let alone the same room… but right now they're battling head to head across a conference table, with the Secretary of State acting as a… global referee."

Ingrid let go of the breath she'd been holding, still unclear how any of that impacted on her. What could she add to any negotiations? She said nothing, hopeful Franklin would get to the point soon. She shifted in her seat and crossed her legs. Out of the corner of her eye, she sensed Angelis lean forward.

"Can I get you anything, Ingrid? Coffee? Water?" he asked.

"I'm perfectly fine, Mr Angelis." She deliberately chose not to use his first name. The point wasn't lost on him. With one eyebrow raised, he leaned back against the cabinet.

"The Secretary of State traveled to France accompanied by her granddaughter," Franklin continued. "Not normal protocol, by any means." He patted the file beneath his hands. "In fact, it's highly irregular and should never have been allowed to happen. But it did." He let out a long, disappointed sigh. "Apparently the girl has been having some… issues at home. She and her parents don't see eye to eye—about very much at all. So I guess her grandmother must have thought it would be a good idea to distract her with a little European high culture."

"And doubtless a lot of shopping," Angelis chimed in.

"Quite possibly. Whether she was in Paris to look at the paintings in the Louvre or the shops along the Avenue Montaigne, is kind of beside the point right now." He stared Ingrid in the eye. "The girl is missing."

SEVEN

Ingrid gazed back at him, speechless and motionless. Her mind was swirling with so many questions she was glad she was sitting down. The girl could have been abducted by any one of a number of organizations: terrorists, any variety of European mafia, from post oligarchy Russian to the old fashioned Sicilian kind, regular domestic criminal extortionists, religious fundamentalists. *Holy crap*. It was a diplomatic disaster.

"Missing?" she finally managed.

"She was assigned a private bodyguard paid for by her grandmother."

"Why weren't Diplomatic Security guarding her?"

"As the girl isn't officially deemed a close relative, the personnel looking after the Secretary of State couldn't be used to protect her granddaughter. The State Secretary can't be seen to be misusing tax payers' money and all. The guard assigned to protect her clearly wasn't up to the job."

"And you think the girl's been abducted?"

Sol Franklin glanced at Angelis. "No, not abducted. It seems Rachel Whitticker deliberately slipped away from her bodyguard some time yesterday evening."

"She did what?"

"Quite determined young thing, it would appear." Angelis ran a hand through his thick quiff. And shook his head. "The tragedy is, Fortnum's has an office in Paris, we could have coordinated the whole thing. If only the Secretary of State had known about us—we wouldn't have let her granddaughter get away." Angelis threw an accusatory stare in Sol Franklin's general direction.

"The French security company was recommended by the Bureau's Chief of Mission in Paris. It's on a list of approved suppliers. We've used their operatives in the past very successfully. That's why we're taking responsibility for—"

"Clearing up the mess?" Angelis said.

Ingrid felt as if she were watching a private fight between the two men. It was unseemly at best and downright unprofessional at worst. She considered wading in and breaking it up, like some teaching assistant in a kindergarten playground. Instead she decided to remind them she was still in the room. "When exactly did all this happen?"

Angelis managed to tear his gaze away from Sol Franklin and finally turned to her. "She gave her incompetent minder the slip shortly before ten p.m. last night."

"How?"

"The bodyguard hasn't been that forthcoming with the details so far," Franklin said. The Regional Security Officer at the embassy in Paris has been questioning her himself. She's injured—slipped off a roof while she was giving chase."

"You're telling me Rachel Whitticker escaped across Parisian rooftops?" Ingrid pictured the architecture of the Paris skyline she remembered from films and postcards.

"It seems the young lady is athletic as well as smart," Franklin said.

"To be fair, it was just the one roof and a series of fire escapes," Angelis added. "But nevertheless, it does seem young Rachel is really quite resourceful."

"I still don't understand what my role is in all this," Ingrid said. "You want me to go France to help the police track her down? Is that even a job for the FBI?"

"It's a little complicated," Sol Franklin said.

"Doesn't the Legal Attaché program have a Bureau agent in the embassy in Paris who can deal with it?"

Sol Franklin held up his hands. "I haven't told you the whole story."

Ingrid uncrossed her legs and leaned forward in her seat, willing him to do just that.

"We're pretty sure she's left France. We believe she's here in the UK."

"She is?"

"It seems she took a Eurostar train out of Paris Gare Du Nord. She arrived at St Pancras International just after eight a.m. this morning."

"If she lost her bodyguard at ten p.m. last night, what has she been doing for the last ten hours?"

"Covering her tracks. We now have CCTV footage confirming her presence at a number of suburban train stations just outside Paris. She left Paris initially on a train headed for Boulogne. Got off first stop she could, then criss-crossed her way back again. Meanwhile, everyone's expecting her to arrive at the Channel to catch a ferry."

"So surely UK Border Control were alerted last night." Ingrid stared at Sol Franklin. He avoided eye contact by looking down at the file in front of him. "I don't understand. Why didn't they just pick her up as soon as her passport was checked this morning?"

"They weren't alerted last night. The French security company thought they could contain the situation. They didn't admit that they'd lost the girl until this morning. After Rachel Whitticker's arrival here."

"That's just crazy. Surely as soon as the Secretary of State was informed of the situation her security detail would have taken over—close relative or not." Ingrid glanced at Angelis. He just stared back at her and said nothing. She got the distinct impression there was a vital fact they weren't sharing with her.

"I need to explain how you can help us in all this." Franklin said.

"Diplomatic Security should be taking control of the situation. I don't even understand why the Bureau has gotten involved."

He grimaced. "The Diplomatic Security Service really have no role to play. Trust me on that."

"Then why not let the UK cops handle it?"

"We'd actually really like to keep the whole situation contained as much as possible. If this thing leaked out to the press… well you can forget about brokering a peace deal in central Africa. All hell would break loose."

"OK… then use whichever agents you have assigned to dealing with this kind of thing, here in London."

Sol Franklin pulled a pack of cigarettes from his shirt pocket and started to push it around his desk like a child playing with a toy car. "As I said before… it's complicated."

"The Bureau agents here are all men and you need a woman to act as chaperone once she's found?" Ingrid couldn't think of another possible explanation for her involvement.

"Not exactly." He slipped the cigarettes back in his pocket. "The FBI has a single dedicated post here at the embassy for dealing with criminal matters. An errant granddaughter on the lam? That's not something for counterterrorism or counterintelligence agents to get involved with. Politically, that would be… inappropriate. So…" He glanced toward Angelis for assistance. Franklin looked like a man in need of saving.

"The agent who previously had the job here is no longer in post. I gather he left in rather a hurry," Angelis said.

"So you want me to do his job until the girl is located?"

Sol Franklin smiled broadly at her. "Precisely."

"Wouldn't it just be easier to bring in some trusted members of the UK security forces? MI5?" She threw Angelis a glowering look. She still didn't understand why an operative from a private security company was so closely involved in the operation. "MI5 wouldn't go running to the press."

"It's not an official matter. We don't want to escalate it to the level of an international incident. Getting MI5 involved would do exactly that," Franklin said and looked at Angelis again. "Which is why we're utilizing the services of Nick's company."

Ingrid sat very still for a few moments and considered everything she'd been told. There still seemed to be a piece of the puzzle missing. "If this girl is smart, resourceful, and clearly determined to pursue her own agenda here in Europe… what's the problem? She'll do whatever it is she came here for then return to Paris, won't she? Why do we have to track her down at all?"

Sol Franklin shifted uncomfortably in his seat. "We can't wait around for her to just turn up. We absolutely must find Rachel Whitticker before the Secretary of State completes today's round of negotiations in Strasbourg—at midnight tonight."

A moment later it dawned on Ingrid what they had been keeping from her.

Sweet Jesus.

She stared first at Angelis then Sol Franklin. "The Secretary of State doesn't even know her granddaughter is missing, does she?"

EIGHT

For a moment, all Ingrid could do was stare into space as she calculated the possible ramifications of not informing the Secretary of State and then not being able to locate the girl. She stopped when her imagination conjured up so much crap hitting the fan they'd need waterproofs and waders.

"You can't keep this from her," Ingrid said. "She has a right to know."

"The Secretary of State is in the middle of very delicate negotiations. We can't risk her being distracted by something this… this…" Sol Franklin was having trouble finding the right word.

"Her eighteen-year-old granddaughter has disappeared—please don't tell me you were going to say *trivial*." Ingrid wondered whether they'd be treading on such sensitive eggshells if the Secretary of

State had been a man. Didn't they think Jayne Whitticker could cope with a family crisis and still do her job? Ingrid decided to keep that observation to herself. It wouldn't help the situation.

"You've got to understand our position here. It's one hell of a judgment call."

"What about the girl's parents? Surely you have to tell them?"

"At the moment," Angelis interjected, "this is all about containment. We need to keep this information as secure as we can."

"Her parents are hardly likely to leak the news to the media," Ingrid said, then immediately realized how wrong she was. Of course they'd go to the papers and the TV stations—anything to get their daughter back. Angelis was about to speak, but Ingrid held up her hand. "It's OK—I know what you're going to say. So—we tell no one. I get that. But what happens when the Secretary of State finally does find out about it?"

"We'll cross that bridge when we have to," Franklin said. "There's a bigger picture here. We have a moral duty to ensure the peace talks continue without interruption."

"After all, as you've already suggested, Rachel Whitticker might be perfectly safe holed up in a five star hotel somewhere, having a lovely time," Angelis said.

"What's she doing for money?" Ingrid asked. "Any recent transactions on her credit card?"

Angelis moved from his spot leaning against the file cabinet to stand beside Sol Franklin. "According to the French bodyguard, the girl was flashing her plastic around with gay abandon in the upmarket Parisian fashion boutiques. She actually used the guard to carry her shopping for her. We've checked with the stores—it seems she used a credit card registered to Jayne Whitticker."

"Her grandmother gave her a card?"

Angelis shrugged.

"You're not suggesting she stole it?"

"Not at all. The Secretary of State just wanted to keep her granddaughter occupied, one supposes."

"And she used the card to pay for her train ticket to London?" Ingrid asked.

"No. The transactions stop after a large withdrawal of cash from an ATM. She's smart enough not to leave a trail."

"So she'll be using that cash in the UK?"

"That's the assumption we're making."

"Same goes for her cell phone—I guess she's not using that either?" Ingrid asked.

"Not a peep from it since last night." Angelis turned around and separated two wooden slats on the window shade. He peered outside. "We really should get going. We have a lot to do."

"When you say 'we' who exactly are you referring to?" Ingrid asked Franklin.

"Nick's company have pretty much come to our rescue. They can provide support on the ground and the intel we need. We can't risk going through Bureau channels to gather intelligence about the girl—it'd raise too many flags right across all the security services.

"I still don't understand why you need me. It sounds as if Mr Angelis' company have things pretty much under control."

"Nick needs a US government agent to work with on the ground. You are the best candidate for the job. If you refuse to help us, well... not to put too fine a point on it..."

"We're a tad screwed." Angelis helpfully finished Franklin's sentence.

"Really?"

"If things go tits up and it's just me and my associates on the case, the fallout—not just for my company, you understand, for the US government too—would be catastrophic. Relying entirely on an outside agency? Our role has to remain completely unofficial throughout."

"Wait a minute." Ingrid wriggled forward on her chair. "Are you saying you want me involved to carry the can if things go wrong?"

Franklin glared at Angelis. "Not at all." He continued to stare at Angelis until the private spook slunk away, back to his original position. "When we find Rachel we need a US government representative present. To act as a chaperone." He smiled resignedly at her. "As one Federal agent to another, I'm asking for your help here."

Ingrid thought about the alternative—returning to the training session in an airless conference room at New Scotland Yard. She pictured all the bored detectives who clearly wanted to be some place else. A thought occurred to her. "If she left Paris last night, how come the Secretary of State didn't miss her? Wouldn't they have spoken on the phone?"

"The negotiations went on well into the early hours. Then resumed at eight a.m. the following morning. The Secretary of State didn't have a chance to miss her," Sol Franklin said.

"Do you have any idea why Rachel Whitticker has come to the UK? Why not hang out in Paris instead?"

"With a babysitter?"

"OK—once she'd shaken off the unwanted companion—she could have gone to Berlin, or Milan, or a half dozen other fabulous European cities. Why London?"

"We've been checking her social media accounts. She's been having a lot of online chats with a particular individual studying at Imperial College in London."

"You've spoken to him?"

"We would if we could. It seems he's disappeared too. Some time last night. None of his college chums have a clue where he might have gone. His mobile phone has been inactive since ten p.m. last night."

Sol Franklin leaned his elbows on his desk. "Can I assume from your questions that you will accept this mission?" He stared her in the eye, long and hard.

Ingrid had to look away. She didn't want to let the Bureau down. But equally, she wasn't keen to spend any more time with Nick Angelis.

"Come on, Agent Skyberg," Franklin said, "you can save the girl and help bring peace to a war-torn region."

Ingrid blinked. The room was suddenly deathly quiet except for the hum and clank of the heating pipes. Even Angelis had wisely decided to hold his tongue. After Franklin had put the mission in such stark terms, how could she refuse?

"OK," she said, "but for God's sake let's not waste any more time."

NINE

Sol Franklin jumped out of his chair, enclosed Ingrid's right hand in both of his and pumped her arm. "Great to have you on board, Ingrid."

"It certainly is." Angelis, for once, stayed back. "Shall we?" He pointed toward the door.

"Wait a second," Franklin said. He opened a drawer beneath his desk and retrieved Ingrid's cell phone. "You might need this."

Ingrid slipped the phone into her purse and got as far as the door when she stopped. "Should I be armed for this mission?"

"UK Home Office don't like us running around with guns," Franklin told her. "There shouldn't be any need for a sidearm anyway. She is just a teenager."

Ingrid walked with Angelis to the elevator in something approaching amicable silence. Just as she was wondering how long it might last, Angelis opened his mouth.

"I suppose you're wondering why we chose you and not your colleague," he said, and punched the 'down' button with a knuckle.

"I hadn't given it any thought," she lied.

"Of course not. You Feds are known for your lack of competitiveness, I was forgetting."

Angelis' sarcasm was going to grow tiresome pretty quickly. She had to nip it in the bud. "If we're going to work together today you can drop the lame attempt at humor."

He raised his eyebrows.

"In case you're wondering, yes I *can* take a joke, but sarcasm is a little beneath you, isn't it?"

"Ouch. You are harsh."

"But fair." Ingrid allowed herself a smile. She decided to change the subject. "So… you've worked with the embassy before?"

"I've lost count of the number of times. Sol Franklin is a very good agent. One of the finest it's been my pleasure to meet." The elevator doors opened. They stepped inside and Angelis hit the button for the first floor. "What I was saying before… aren't you even mildly curious?"

"I'm sorry?"

"You're fooling no one with this innocent act. You're dying to know why we chose you instead of your colleague. Admit it."

Ingrid shrugged. Of course she wanted to know what she'd done right. A little positive appraisal was always welcome, no matter how long you'd been on the job. But she sure as hell wasn't going to give him the satisfaction of letting him know he was right.

"Sol and I agreed that agent Gardiner didn't seem to be in the right… mental state to take on an active mission. She seemed rather preoccupied. About her children and so on. Wouldn't actually shut up about them, in fact, would she?"

"You were listening to our private conversation?"

"I'm sure that doesn't surprise you. You seemed to adapt quickly to the possibility of surveillance. You barely said a word all the time you were in there. You kept your own counsel magnificently well."

The elevator doors opened and they made their way down a long corridor toward the main entrance.

"Where are we headed?" Ingrid asked Angelis when they'd exited the embassy compound.

"Imperial College—I thought we'd put some pressure on the friends of Rachel Whitticker's online chum. See what we can winkle out of them."

"I thought you said they were refusing to speak."

"That's why we need to exert some pressure."

"Seriously? Is that all you have? Some guy Rachel Whitticker spoke to online is your only lead?"

"It took our tech people a while to uncover his identity. The girl's been covering her tracks extraordinarily well."

It didn't seem to Ingrid that Fortnum Security's intelligence gathering capabilities were up to the job. Surely the Bureau could find a better option. "What did the French bodyguard tell you? Anything we can use?"

"Unsurprisingly, she's been saying very little. Whether she's trying to save her own skin or protect her company, is not entirely clear. We should learn from her example, however. Never underestimate a determined teenager." He laid a hand on Ingrid's arm and steered her to the left. "I've parked the bike on the other side of Grosvenor Square."

"Bike?"

"Motorcycle, naturally—I don't expect you to balance on the handlebars of a bicycle! It's the best way to get around town."

Ingrid pulled her arm away from his grasp.

"You have ridden pillion on a motorcycle before, I take it?"

"I'm more used to riding solo."

"You're a biker? I didn't read that in your Bureau profile. How simply delicious. Now I know we'll have some fun."

Ingrid wondered at Angelis' way of speaking. What was this guy on? At times he sounded like some flamboyant dandy from a period drama. "Fun? We have a job to do—helping promote world peace, remember?"

"I'm sure you weren't taken in by Sol's spin any more than I was."

Just as they were about to walk through the entrance to Grosvenor Square, which to Ingrid's eye was basically a patch of frozen grass criss-crossed with cinder paths, a woman and a man started to rush toward them.

"I know you!" the woman said, pointing a finger at Ingrid.

Ingrid looked the woman up and down. She'd been in the embassy earlier, attempting to get her press accreditation approved. *Great*—that was all they needed, a curious journalist latching onto them.

"Get a couple of shots of these two, Frank," she ordered the overweight, disheveled man standing next to her. Immediately he raised the camera that was hanging around his neck and clicked. The flash temporarily burned on Ingrid's retinas. "Can you tell me what your business was in the embassy earlier, Agent..."

Nice try. Ingrid started to turn away.

"Does it have anything to do with the Secretary of State's impending visit? Expecting trouble? Is the embassy recruiting extra manpower? They seemed super keen on getting your ID sorted out in a hurry." She turned her attention to Angelis. "And who are you?"

"You'll have to delete those photographs," Angelis told the photographer, ignoring the woman's questions completely.

The overweight man clutched the camera to his chest. "It's a free country."

"You're English? Working out of the American embassy?" The journalist stepped so close to Angelis, Ingrid thought the woman might bump right into him. "There has to be a story in that. Who do you work for, the Met, MI5, MI6?"

Angelis' hand was outstretched toward the camera. "Either I watch you delete the images or I get a very amenable policeman to confiscate the camera." He glanced around. "Oh look—there's a cop just over there. He looks bored. Shall we give him a little something to do?"

The photographer looked first at the policeman, who was sitting astride a motorcycle, then at the journalist. "Don't look at me like that," he said, "it could take me all bloody week to get this back." He pulled the strap over his head and showed Angelis the screen. Then he scrolled through the images, hitting the delete button for each of them.

"There," Angelis said, when the process was over, "that wasn't so bad, was it?"

"You do realize your actions have only served to reinforce my hunch?" the reporter said.

"I have no idea what you're talking about." Angelis grabbed Ingrid's arm again. She was getting a little tired of it.

"If you hadn't overreacted like that, I might have decided hanging around the embassy had been a waste of time—freezing off my whatnots in the sleeting wind for no good reason." She thrust out her hand at Ingrid. "Angela Tate, Senior Political Editor at the *Evening News*. I expect we'll meet again."

Angelis practically dragged Ingrid away across the square. The only thing that stopped her yanking her arm away from him again was the photo opportunity it might give the photographer. Angelis didn't speak again until they'd reached the other side of Grosvenor Square. "Jesus Christ that woman doesn't let up."

"You know her?"

"Only by reputation. Once she sinks her teeth into a story, she won't let go until she's made it onto the front page."

Great. Ingrid hoped they didn't bump into Tate again.

When they finally reached Angelis' motorcycle, Ingrid discovered it was a classic old Ducati. Immediately she was envious. She had a Harley at home, and was so fiercely loyal to the company she'd even bought shares in it. But there was something about the curve and the line of these Italian bikes that she'd admired for as long as she'd been riding.

"Impressed?"

"Not too bad."

He smiled at her and unlocked a large storage box on the back of the bike. He handed her a shiny white helmet with a tinted visor.

"So, imagine, if you can, that you're an eighteen-year-old American, a stranger in London, about to meet your online 'lover' in the flesh for the first time—"

"We don't know that—maybe they've met before."

"It's her first trip to Europe and, according to US Homeland Security, he's never been to America." He shoved his motorcycle helmet over his extravagant quiff. "If we assume the two lovebirds are holed up together somewhere, where do we start looking?"

"You've checked out his home?"

"He lives in halls. Not the most salubrious location to impress a girl."

"What about his folks' place?"

"We've had their house under surveillance for a couple of hours. There's been no sign of him. Besides, he wouldn't go somewhere so obvious."

"Would he even expect anyone would be looking?"

"He might not, but she would."

"Maybe they've eloped—isn't there some place in Scotland where people do that?"

"Elopement? My, Agent Skyberg, I didn't have you pegged as a romantic."

"I didn't realize you'd judged me already."

"Oh yes. The moment I first saw you."

TEN

They checked in with the registrar's office at Imperial College in South Kensington, and headed straight to the math department of the 19th century college campus, assured by the clerk in the office that the student's friends were just finishing up a lecture on vector calculus.

"Seems he's quite a geek," Angelis commented, mild disgust in his tone.

"Nothing wrong with that."

"Try telling that to the unfortunate individuals who have been afflicted with an obsession with Star Trek and The Hobbit."

"It's not a disease." Ingrid noticed the unexpected passion in her voice only as the words left her mouth.

"Do I detect an element of defensiveness, agent? Surely you don't expect me to believe you were ever a bespectacled swot?"

Ingrid chose not to answer. Instead she said, "What's our cover story with the students here?"

"Same as it was with the registrar's office. An American girl is missing and the embassy—at the behest of her parents—is doing all it can to track her down."

"But these students might actually know her name. If her online pal has spoken to his friends about her."

"Not her real name—the story would be all over social media by now if anyone was aware of her true identity."

They reached the lecture hall and slipped in quietly just as the lecturer was giving the students their assignment for the holidays. As far as Ingrid could tell, it was an impenetrable algebraic formula that Einstein himself would have struggled with. She'd majored in languages. Applied math was definitely not her strong point.

Angelis strode toward the lectern, had a very brief and quiet word with the lecturer, then leaned close to the microphone. His voice boomed through the hall as soon as he started speaking. He quickly pulled back from the mic. Before he had a chance to resume, the students started to get to their feet. "Sit down!" he bellowed. Immediately the entire audience dropped back into their seats. "Thank you. I promise to keep you just a few moments." He surveyed the hall, smiling all the time. "My colleague and I are very interested in speaking to anyone who knows a Mr

Adam Oxley. Please make your way in an orderly fashion to the front of the room." He stood back and waited as the majority of the students shuffled right out of the lecture theater.

After a little while the hall was empty, save for only a handful of students dotted around in far flung seats. It didn't seem the young student was exactly popular among his peers.

Angelis clapped his hands together. "Come on, then. Don't be shy. Come down to the front row, would you? This is a private conversation, after all. I wouldn't want to broadcast it."

Reluctantly, all five students—three boys and two girls—slouched toward the front and slumped into seats that still allowed for some distance between them.

"You can do better than that. You two move in."

Ingrid patiently waited for Angelis to rearrange the small group, conscious time was slipping away.

"What's this about?" one of the male students asked Angelis. "What's Adam supposed to have done?"

"Whoa! Back up. You're getting way ahead of yourself. As far as we're aware, Mr Oxley has done nothing wrong. We're just interested in having a little chat with him."

"And you are?"

Ingrid stepped forward. She held up her badge and explained who she was and where she was from.

"The American embassy? What's that got to do with Adam?" The vocal student's friend nudged him in the ribs.

"We haven't seen Adam for a couple of days," the rib-nudger said.

Angelis turned his attention to him. "Do you know where he might have taken himself off to?"

"Have you tried his parents' house?" the student suggested.

"He's not at home with them."

"Maybe he's having an early Christmas break somewhere."

"You still haven't explained why the American embassy is involved," the first student said.

Ingrid and Angelis exchanged a glance.

"We'll get on to that," Angelis said. "How did Adam seem, the last time you saw him?"

"Seem?"

"Happy, sad, distracted, excited. I'm looking for an appropriate adjective."

"He just seemed like Adam. A bit miserable, but basically OK."

Ingrid noticed the two female students had said nothing. They were sitting next to one another, but the one on the left was leaning away slightly from the girl next to her. She seemed keen to keep her distance.

Angelis pulled a folded sheet of paper from his pocket. He carefully unfolded it and smoothed it out on his thigh. He showed it to the male students. "We believe Adam may know where this young woman is. We need to speak to him urgently to find out."

"Who is she?" The vocal male student plucked the color copy of a head and shoulders shot of Rachel Whitticker from Angelis' grasp.

"We believe she's a very close friend of Adam's," Angelis said.

"She also happens to be a US citizen, which is why the embassy is involved," Ingrid explained. "This girl has gone missing and her parents are desperate to ensure she's safe."

"'Very close' friend," the rib-nudger repeated. "You mean like, girlfriend?" He managed to tear his gaze from the portrait of the young woman with the long brown tresses, hazel eyes and full pink lips, to glance briefly up at one of the female students. She glared back at him.

"She may be his girlfriend," Angelis said.

"No way," the third male student said, finally joining the discussion. "She's far too fit for Adam. No way could he pull someone as gorgeous as that."

The female student continued to glare at him. The one who was trying to keep her distance stared down at the floor.

"You really work for the FBI?" The third student turned to Ingrid, his face a mask of suspicion.

"That's right, sir."

"Then tell us why you're really here," the first student chimed in.

"I'm sorry?"

"You come here spinning us an unbelievable story about Adam, and expect us to just swallow it? What's the real reason for your visit?"

Good grief. A hundred and fifty students in that hall and they'd managed to hook themselves a real live conspiracy theorist.

The glaring female student was craning her neck to get a glimpse of the photograph. Ingrid nudged Angelis' arm. He grabbed the picture back and handed it to her.

"She is beautiful," the girl said. "I knew Adam had moved on after I dumped him, but I had no idea his little trans-Atlantic boffin friend was anything special."

Ingrid detected a definite hint of jealousy in the girl's tone. "You used to date Adam?"

"We split up during the summer vacation."

"And you know about her?" Ingrid pointed to the picture.

"He's been really secretive lately. At first I'd assumed he was seeing someone else on campus."

The girl sitting next to her shifted forward in her seat, like a woman poised to make a swift exit.

"I'd seen details of her profile before, but never her picture," the first girl continued. "I know Adam was quite smitten with her."

"Do you know how they met?"

"Some online forum—for geniuses, Adam liked to pretend. You have to pass a test before you can make any posts—to prove your IQ is above 175."

"That's high, is it?" Angelis asked, a little disingenuously, Ingrid suspected. He must have known it was damn high.

"We think maybe they've taken off together. You know—a romantic few nights alone," Angelis said.

"Yeah, right," the conspiracy theorist muttered. "In his dreams."

"For the sake of argument, let's just assume Mr Oxley has managed to woo this attractive young lady.

Where might he have taken her?" Angelis looked directly toward Oxley's ex-girlfriend, who wriggled in her seat. "Is there any place you visited with Adam, any place he might have taken her?"

The girl took a deep breath. "Last summer we went to his grandmother's house—she wasn't there, she's dead. It's in the middle of the country somewhere."

"Where?" Angelis asked. He grabbed his cell phone from a pocket and was poised to type the address into his GPS app.

"For God's sake, Sara! Don't tell them anything else—we don't even know if we can trust them," the conspiracy theorist warned.

"Oh grow up!" The girl thought for a moment. "Essex," she said, emphatically.

"Can you be a little more specific? It is rather a large county," Angelis said.

"His parents dropped us off there and picked us up again. I never really paid attention. I'm sorry, but I don't know the address."

A second or two later the girl next to her slowly got to her feet. In barely more than a whisper, she said, "I know. I know where it is."

ELEVEN

The ex-girlfriend stood up too, her face just inches away from the other girl's. "How? How can you possibly know…" Her eyes opened wide. "Wait a second, are you saying you've been seeing Adam?"

The quiet girl looked at her shoes and said nothing.

"I thought you were supposed to be my friend."

"You weren't interested in him anymore." She sniffed, almost defiantly. "Besides, it only lasted a few weeks. Until he became besotted with Sophie."

Ingrid and Angelis exchanged a glance. *Sophie*?

"There is such a thing as loyalty, you know."

Angelis cleared his throat noisily. "Forgive me for interrupting your important conversation, ladies, but we are rather keen to track this Adam chap down." He touched the quiet girl very gently on the arm. She pulled away as if she'd been scolded. "So you know where Adam's grandmother's house is, do you?"

"Not the exact address. But I know it's in a village called Bicknacre."

"Do you know if Adam's grandmother was his dad's or mom's mom?" Ingrid asked her.

She blinked back at her. "I… I don't see… I don't know…"

"His dad's mum," the other girl interjected and stuck her chin in the air, obviously pleased she knew Adam Oxley better than her friend.

"Thank you." Ingrid moved between the two girls. "Listen, I can't even begin to tell you how important it is that we find… Sophie. She's young, a long way from home… she's really quite vulnerable. Her parents are out of their minds with worry. Is there any place else you can think of Adam may have taken her? Maybe a favorite hotel? Here in London or in another city?"

"He's not really a champagne and roses, posh hotel kind of bloke," his ex said. She looked to her friend for agreement.

"It's true. Adam's a bit… careful with money. He wouldn't splash out, no matter how besotted he was. When it comes down to it, he's just too… sensible for grand romantic gestures."

Ingrid wondered if Oxley might be swayed if someone else was paying. She hadn't yet discovered just how much cash Rachel Whitticker had withdrawn from the ATM in Paris.

"Anything else you can tell us about the vanishing Mr Oxley?" Angelis asked the male students.

All three students adjusted their postures, two folding their arms across their chests defiantly, the third deliberately turning away.

"Thank you so much for your cooperation," Angelis said, "if you do think of anything that might help us find Adam, please, don't hesitate to call me." He handed each of them a business card.

Ingrid watched the three male students shuffle out the lecture hall, followed by the two girls, who seemed to be chatting quite happily to one another, clearly united against a common enemy.

Once they were all gone, Ingrid said, "Let's hope the old lady never remarried."

"I'm sorry?" Angelis was staring down at the smiling face of Rachel Whitticker. He refolded the color photocopy and shoved it back in a pocket.

"Your company's got access to a whole range of national databases, right?"

"Our intel is second only to Mossad's."

"Great—then you should have no problem finding a property in Essex originally registered to a Mr Oxley."

"I like your thinking." Angelis retrieved his phone and put in a hurried call to his company headquarters. When he hung up he said, "Should have the GPS coordinates for us in a couple of minutes."

They hurried out of the math department and back toward Angelis' motorcycle.

"You think it's worth traveling to this Bicknacre place?" Ingrid asked him. "Do you have any other leads at all?"

"Rachel's been very clever covering her tracks. We've still got people working on it, but right now, it's Adam Oxley or bust."

"How long to get to Essex?"

"Too long. Even on the bike."

"Can we justify the expense of a helicopter?" Ingrid broke into a jog to match Angelis' long-legged stride. "Actually, I never asked, who is funding this mission?"

"My company is providing our services for free. We generally like to keep our regular clients happy. These are quite extraordinary circumstances. But a chopper? That might be a generous donation too far."

Angelis' phone bleeped. He glanced down at it. "We have our address."

Ingrid slowed down a little, conscious they were rushing at something that maybe needed more consideration.

Angelis picked up her change of pace and slowed too. "What is it?"

"Let's think about this for a second."

"I'm listening."

"What if they're not in Essex? They could quite easily be holed up in a hotel right here in London. We don't really have the time to waste visiting some little village in the middle of nowhere just to find out the house is empty."

They reached the motorcycle.

Angelis pulled out the motorcycle helmets from the box on the back of the bike. "I can hardly ask the Essex police to check the property out for us. We do have to keep this thing under wraps."

"You don't have operatives all over the country you can call on?"

"Fortnum's is a big operation, but it's not that big."

"OK—we contact someone else. We just need a damn good cover story."

"Have anything in mind?"

"Sure. Find me a lawyer close to those GPS coordinates."

"Oh I think I like where this is going."

Two minutes later Ingrid was on hold at Simons and Atkins in Chelmsford, Essex. Just a few miles from the village of Bicknacre. Eventually the receptionist put her through to one of the junior partners, a Mr Jennings.

"How can I help you, madam?"

"Good afternoon. I'm calling from… Weinstein and Zeigler in New York, we're trying to track down the beneficiaries of a sizable inheritance. The last known address we have is a small village a few miles from your office."

"Really? Which one?" Mr Jennings said, a definite note of excitement in his voice.

Angelis leaned on the bike and folded his arms. He was making faces at her.

Ingrid turned away. She didn't need the distraction. "A place named Bicknacre. Unfortunately all our letters have been ignored. We really would like to tie things up."

"You'd like us to speak to the beneficiary?"

"Right now just knowing that we have the right address for him would be good. It's a Mr Adam Oxley."

"How about I visit the property myself?"

"Would you? That's just great."

"I'd need to check with my secretary, but I'm sure I have a slot in my diary some time next week."

Ingrid rolled her eyes. "I was hoping you could go there right now."

"Oh no, that won't be possible. I'm afraid we do things a little differently here in the UK."

Ingrid sucked in a breath, wondering if that meant slowly and inefficiently. "What about sending a clerk? We just need to find out if Mr Oxley is actually resident at the property. At this stage, we'd rather no one made direct contact with him." Ingrid was keen that if Adam Oxley and Rachel Whitticker were at Oxley's grandmother's house, they should remain blissfully ignorant that they were even close to being discovered.

"I suppose I could ask Marjorie, our receptionist, to swing by in her lunch break."

"That would be very kind of you. If it's not too much trouble." Ingrid gave the lawyer her contact details and was assured Marjorie would call her back within the hour. He was also very clear just how much Marjorie's time would be charged out at. As soon as she hung up, Ingrid explained the situation to Angelis.

"So—as we have an hour or so to kill," he said, once she'd finished, "how about a bite to eat?"

TWELVE

The bite to eat turned into a rushed three course lunch at Angelis' private members' club in a street named Pall Mall. The street was lined on both sides by impressive Regency houses, and looked so familiar to Ingrid she guessed it must have been used as a location for countless period films and TV dramas.

On the way to his club, Angelis had ensured they rode slowly past Buckingham Palace. The golden statue of an angel on top of the Victoria Memorial glinted in the weak December sun. Ingrid had seen nothing like it before. She hoped she'd get a chance to do some decent sightseeing before she returned home.

In the lull between main and dessert courses, Angelis leaned back in his chair and gestured extravagantly around the large banqueting room, complete with oil paintings on the walls and crystal chandeliers hanging from the high ceilings. "What do you think of the place? Impressive, isn't it?"

Ingrid shrugged. "I guess."

"You guess? Have you any idea just how exclusive this establishment is? I had to wait a bloody long time to be accepted as a member."

"Hey, at least they let you in eventually." Ingrid forced a smile. The more he tried to impress her, the greater her determination not to show any interest. "I've been thinking, what if Rachel Whitticker isn't actually with this Oxley guy in deepest darkest Essex? We have assumed they're together."

"I don't think we've assumed anything at all. I'm keeping an open mind."

"But according to the intel, he remains your only lead right now."

Angelis gave her a begrudging nod.

"What if she booked herself into a hotel right here in London? Shouldn't we at least be checking out that possibility?"

"How do you propose we do that?"

"How much cash did she withdraw from the Paris ATM?"

"Seven hundred Euros."

"That's enough for a last minute ticket on the Eurostar and what else? One night in a five star hotel?"

"Five star? Barely."

"Can you really see the Secretary of State's granddaughter wanting to stay anywhere else?"

"Where are you going with this?"

"Your company must have the resources to visit them all—maybe some upmarket four star hotels too. Have a discreet chat with the managers, find out if any eighteen-year-old girls checked in without a lot of baggage today."

"That's an awful lot of hotels."

"Start with the most famous." Ingrid pushed away her plate and what was left of her poached salmon salad. "I really don't feel comfortable relying on a single lead. Time's running out. We need a contingency."

Angelis grudgingly agreed to call head office and line up the manpower to do what Ingrid had suggested. He was still on the phone when the receptionist from the Essex lawyers' office called Ingrid.

"Miss Skyberg?" The woman's voice seemed a little hesitant. Ingrid wondered if maybe she was worried about the cost of calling an American cell phone. "I visited the house in Bicknacre and spoke to the young man."

Goddammit. Ingrid had specifically requested they didn't talk to him. He could be halfway to Scotland by now. Or any other goddamn place "What did you say to him?"

"Oh don't worry—I pretended to be an estate agent, asking whether he'd ever considered putting the property on the market."

Ingrid felt a little guilty she'd been so quick to assume the woman was incompetent. "And how did he respond?"

"He told me the house belongs to his parents. It was his grandmother's. He seemed very young to be living there all by himself."

"You didn't see anyone else at the property?"

"We had the conversation on the doorstep, so I can't really say one way or the other. I just got the impression he was alone. He looked a bit… unkempt."

"Thank you so much for your help. It's greatly appreciated." Ingrid hung up. "I forgot to mention before—the lawyers will be invoicing your company for her time," she told Angelis. She decided not to mention the amount.

Angelis gulped down the last of his dessert, something called Eton Mess—a mixture of strawberries, meringue and cream all squished up in a dish. "So, swift visit to Bicknacre for us then."

"How about you make a quick call to your tech guys? See if they've uncovered any more promising leads for us."

Angelis shrugged. "Not necessary. They'd call me if they found anything."

Ingrid was acutely aware time was ticking down. Angelis seemed far too relaxed about everything. They had less than ten hours to locate Rachel Whitticker and pick her up. As far as Ingrid was concerned, they were nowhere near that objective. "But we can travel via helicopter?"

"If I can swing it with the powers that be. Leave it with me." Over coffee Angelis made several calls, each conversation more heated than the one before. Despite her better judgment, Ingrid was actually impressed by his powers of persuasion.

A half hour later they were ducking their heads beneath the downdraft of the rotor blades of the Eurocopter EC120 at a helipad just south of the River Thames in Battersea.

"You've got to admit," Angelis hollered as they boarded, "I do know how to travel in style."

Ingrid buckled up and prepared herself for what the pilot promised would be a bumpy ride.

The journey was mercifully without incident and the helicopter touched down in a farmer's field near the village of Bicknacre just twenty-five minutes later. A taxi was waiting with its engine running in the dirt track that ran along one side of the field.

"Mr Oxley better bloody well be there when we arrive," Angelis said as the cab bumped along the track.

"Let's hope his beautiful new girlfriend is with him."

The taxi pulled in toward the curb twenty or so yards from the dinky little cottage. After giving the driver strict instructions to stay exactly where he was if he expected to get paid, Ingrid and Angelis climbed out and made their way down the narrow road.

The cottage was set apart from the other properties on the street, on its own little patch of land. Even though the day was gloomy, there were no lights on inside.

"You think the woman from the lawyers office spooked him so much he fled?" Ingrid asked as they pushed through the blue painted wooden gate.

"One way to find out." Angelis strode up the brick-paved snaking path and lifted a fist toward the front door.

Ingrid grabbed his arm before he made contact. "Maybe we shouldn't announce our arrival."

"What are you suggesting? Picking the lock?"

"Can you?"

"I have many skills, but I'm afraid that isn't one of them."

Ingrid peered toward the right hand edge of the cottage. "The path probably goes all the way around to the backyard. I'll find a way in through the rear door." She started to move off, but Angelis tugged on her jacket.

"I'll take the back door. Don't even think about arguing with me. I absolutely insist. Give me a couple of minutes."

Ingrid watched Angelis disappear around the side of the building. A few moments later she heard the crash of breaking glass. A moment or two after that she heard what sounded like the thump of footsteps coming down a flight of stairs. The front door swung wide open. Ingrid was suddenly face to face with a skinny boy dressed in low slung jeans and a hooded sweat top. He looked at her through big round glasses, his floppy dark hair falling over his eyes. He glanced left then right.

"If you're thinking of trying to get past me, I suggest you think again." She took a step forward. "I can't let that happen." She lifted a foot over the threshold, forcing the young man further back inside the house.

"Shit!" Oxley turned quickly and started to run. Straight into the open arms of Nick Angelis.

THIRTEEN

"Careful," Angelis said, grabbing the youth's shoulders and pushing him away a few inches to focus more closely on his face. "You might do yourself an injury." He smiled. "And we wouldn't want that, would we? At least, not yet." He forcibly turned Oxley around, slipping a restraining arm across his shoulders, then guided him down the narrow, dark hall to an open door at the other end.

Ingrid pushed open the only other door on the lower floor. It led into a small, gloomy, sparsely furnished living room. No sign of Rachel Whitticker. She then bounded up a flight of creaking wooden stairs to the upper floor. One by one, she kicked open the three doors leading off the hall. Both bedrooms and the bathroom were empty. Rachel had never set foot inside.

Ingrid trundled back downstairs and hurried along the dark hallway. Beyond the door at the other end was a small kitchen. Adam Oxley was sitting on a hard wooden chair next to a table covered in an incongruously cheerful red and white check tablecloth. Angelis was leaning over him, one hand resting on the table. He glanced up at Ingrid, who shook her head.

"Now," Angelis said, "I wouldn't want to keep you for any longer than necessary. Certainly I don't want to waste more of my own time on this… matter. So I have one simple question for you."

Adam Oxley, his eyes wide, stared intensely up at Angelis. He gulped noisily.

"Tell me where your online friend, Sophie, has taken herself off to."

Oxley dropped his gaze to the table. "I don't know what you're talking about. I don't know anyone called Sophie."

"I do hope you're not planning to continue in this vein. I'll tire of it very rapidly. You really don't want to piss me off." He grabbed the boy's hair and yanked back his head. "Shall we try that again?"

Ingrid was just a few feet away. She leaned forward. Angelis must have sensed her movement, because he quickly let go of the boy's head. She was happy to let him continue with the interrogation, but she'd step in as soon as he crossed the line. Right now she hadn't decided exactly where that line was.

"Where is your little friend, Sophie?" Angelis asked again.

"Who are you?" Oxley tried to get to his feet. Angelis quickly clamped a hand on each of the boy's narrow shoulders and forced him back down.

"It doesn't matter who I am."

"You have no right to trespass like this. It's a private property. You broke in." Oxley swiveled in his seat and turned toward Ingrid. "You've no right to be here. I'm going to call the police."

"Feisty little bastard, aren't you?" Angelis swiped a hand close to the boy's head.

Oxley jumped violently in his seat.

"Right, this may be the very last time I ask you nicely. "Where is she?"

"I don't know who you're talking about!"

Without another word, Angelis marched across the room and opened a wooden cabinet beneath the sink. He crouched low and peered inside. Then quickly stood up and spun around. "You do know we have the power to arrest you? Keep you in custody indefinitely, using America's Patriot Act. The US really doesn't like anyone messing with their citizens." Angelis turned back to the cabinet, pulled out a large orange bucket and shoved it in the sink. "Or I could cut to the chase and bring alleged US interrogation techniques right here into your late departed grandmother's kitchen." He turned on the faucet, water spluttered and gushed into the bucket.

"What are you doing?" the boy asked and attempted to stand again.

"Sit down!" Angelis barked.

Oxley slumped back into his seat.

As Ingrid watched the bucket fill, she wondered just how far Nick Angelis would be prepared to go to get the information he wanted. After all, she didn't even know the man. He had to be bluffing. Didn't he?

Angelis glanced over his shoulder at Oxley. "You're a mathematician, you must know all about odds and probabilities. Right now, I'm increasing the likelihood of you giving me what I need." He shot a warning glance in Ingrid's direction, clearly letting her know she shouldn't interfere. "Perhaps I should give you a brief resumé, Adam. Let you know what my credentials are in this… area of expertise." He turned off the faucet and heaved the overflowing bucket out of the sink. In two strides he reached the table and slammed down the bucket, water slopping over the edge, soaking the red and white check tablecloth. "I was once in the army. Did active duty in Iraq, among other places." He took off his jacket and hung it carefully over the back of the chair opposite Oxley. "I've had a great deal of experience with reticent witnesses." He unbuttoned his cuffs.

Ingrid thought she heard the boy whimper. She silently watched Angelis start to roll up his left sleeve, inch by inch, revealing an elaborate tattoo of a woman in a flowing thigh length dress, a quiver of arrows slung over her back, a hunting dog at her feet. Some kind of ancient Greek Goddess, Ingrid supposed. Given Angelis' expensive taste in suits, precisely coiffured hair and upperclass accent, the tattoo was entirely unexpected. She really didn't know what to make of him at all.

"In my experience," Angelis said, "they soon discover the error of their ways and see the light." He grabbed the boy under the arms and dragged him out of his chair. "Usually shortly before everything goes black."

Ingrid stepped a little closer. She was rewarded with another warning glance from Angelis.

With one hand still under the boy's arm, Angelis pushed his face very close to Oxley's. "Where is your American friend?"

"I don't know." Oxley stared at the bucket full of water, a look of terror in his eyes.

"You're prepared to put yourself through all of this to protect some girl you barely know? I'm not sure whether I should applaud your loyalty or despise your stupidity."

Angelis grabbed the boy's neck and pushed his head toward the bucket. Ingrid grabbed Angelis' other arm. He forcefully shook her off.

"Please! I don't know!" Oxley cried.

Angelis shoved Oxley's face into the water. The boy's arms started to flail uselessly at his sides.

"For God's sake!" Ingrid put a hand on Angelis' shoulder.

A few moments later Angelis loosened his grip and the boy reared backward, coughing and spluttering. "Please… don't hurt me," he finally managed to say. "How can I tell you something I don't know?"

Angelis tightened his hold again and applied downward pressure. Oxley's face was just an inch or two from the surface of the water. "Tell me everything you do know!" Angelis pushed him closer, a quarter inch at a time.

Ingrid hesitated. She wanted to stop Angelis, yet at the same time was eager for Oxley to give up any information he might have. She laid a hand on Angelis' arm. "No more."

"Don't make me fight you as well as him," Angelis warned and pushed down Oxley's head another half inch until his nose and mouth were again submerged. Angelis maintained that position for five, ten, fifteen seconds, then finally loosened his hold.

Oxley burst away from the water and sucked down breaths, coughing violently between each one.

"I can do this all day," Angelis told him. "Can you?"

"Please… I really don't know much."

Angelis pushed him back down onto the chair. "I'm listening."

"Sophie told me she was coming to London. She asked me to do her a favor." He wiped a sleeve across his damp face. "She said I should disappear for a few days. Not tell anyone where I was going. Not use my phone. Not talk to anyone about her."

"Did you ask why?"

Oxley shook his head. "I wanted to help her. I like her. She's my friend."

"Didn't what she was asking you to do seem a little odd? Weren't you at least curious?"

"If a friend asks for a favor, you don't start questioning them. You just do it."

"She's your friend, yet she comes all this way and doesn't want to see you. Seems to me she's abused your trust."

"You don't understand. What we've got between us is… special."

"Did she come here to meet someone else?"

"She didn't say. But I suppose it's possible."

"Do you know where she was planning on meeting them?" Ingrid finally felt able to join the conversation. She was still shaken after watching Angelis' performance. How could she just stand back and do nothing to stop him? What had gotten into her? She glanced at her hand. It was trembling.

Oxley shook his head. "She never told me anything about what she was planning to do." He glanced down at the bucket of water. "I swear that's the truth."

"Has she ever mentioned any place here in the UK that might be important to her? Some place she wanted to visit?"

The boy shrugged. "Apart from London, she only ever talked about Cambridge. I want to do my masters there. Sophie said maybe she could come and study there at the same time. She said she absolutely loved the place. Apparently her dad was a student there years back."

"You think she could be there right now?" Ingrid asked.

Oxley coughed before he answered. Water was running out both his nostrils. "I truly don't know. She never gave me any details."

"Does she know anyone there?"

"Some old friends of the family. She said I'd love them. Said they were a bit eccentric… like me."

Adam Oxley hadn't struck Ingrid as the eccentric type. She wondered if Rachel Whitticker had bothered to get to know him online very much at all.

"Which college in Cambridge did her father attend?" Angelis asked. Oxley flinched slightly at the sound of his voice.

"I… I… er…" The boy blinked rapidly, as if he were desperately trying to remember. "King's," he finally blurted out.

"Thank you." Angelis said and carried the bucket over to the sink and emptied it. "It would have been so much easier for both of us if you'd told me that at the start."

FOURTEEN

Ingrid was relieved to discover the taxi was still waiting for them when they pushed through the little blue wooden gate and back onto the street. Fumes from the taxi's exhaust pipe were condensing in the freezing December air.

They walked the twenty or so yards back to the dark blue mini-van in silence. Ingrid was still too mad at Angelis to speak to him. Adam Oxley hadn't deserved that kind of treatment. He was only trying to keep a promise to his friend—however misplaced that loyalty was. She hoped he'd get over the traumatic experience without any lasting effects. But it was quite possible the kid would suffer from some kind of post traumatic stress. *Poor bastard.*

Before they'd left him sitting in a daze at the table, his clothes completely drenched, Ingrid had insisted

Oxley call his parents. His mom agreed to come pick him up later in the day. Hopefully he'd be able to get himself together before she arrived.

They reached the taxi. Angelis opened a rear passenger door and stood aside. Ingrid ignored him and clambered into the car using the other door.

"Oh, please. How long do you intend to keep this up?" he asked.

Ingrid squeezed her hands into tight fists and concentrated on her breathing. She was so close to screaming at him she was concerned the taxi driver would throw her out of the car if she really let rip.

Angelis climbed into the taxi and slammed his door. "I only did what I had to. Call Sol Franklin if you're feeling so squeamish—I'm sure he'll back me up."

Ingrid snatched down as deep a breath as she could then said, "And where exactly did it get us? We're no nearer finding her than we were an hour ago." She glanced at her watch. It was already a quarter before three. The sky was darkening. It looked like a storm was heading in their direction.

"We know we should head for Cambridge. It'll take no time at all in the chopper."

"Do we?"

"She has a connection there."

"According to Adam Oxley."

"I really don't think he was lying to us."

"No—but she lied to him."

"What?"

"She 'absolutely adores' Cambridge? She's never set foot in the country before. And why would she want to visit her dad's friends? She hates anything to do with the guy."

"You think she gave Oxley false information so that he'd pass it on to us?"

"She's smart—we've established that. Why not throw anyone who might be looking for her off the scent?"

"Devious bloody cow."

"We can't risk going to Cambridge. We don't have time to squander on wild goose chases."

"I am very well aware of that fact—but thank you so much for reminding me." He grabbed the back of the driver's seat and leaned forward "What are you waiting for?"

The taxi driver shrugged. "You're seriously considering flying in that?" He wagged a finger at the windshield and the gathering dark clouds beyond. "Rather you than me." He started the engine and quickly pulled out into the empty road.

Angelis got out his phone and tapped the screen two or three times. Then he drummed his fingers on his knee as he waited for someone to pick up. "Hi, yes, it's me. Found anything interesting? Nothing at all? Well, dig a little deeper. See if you can find any connection to Cambridge. Call me back if you find anything. No matter how seemingly insignificant." He made another call. "Anything?" he said without introduction as soon as his call connected. "Keep me posted." He shoved the phone in his pocket. "Seems our girl is rather a whizz at covering her tracks electronically. Unfortunately. Plus there's no news on the five star hotel front." He pushed a hand through the thick mop of hair piled on top of his head. "So… if not Cambridge, where?"

"I can't believe she'd cross the Channel from France and want to be any place except London."

"And you're basing that theory on what exactly?"

Ingrid dropped her voice to a whisper, aware the taxi driver might be listening in. "Trying to think like the eighteen-year-old granddaughter of the Secretary of State."

"Well that's where you have the advantage over me. My feeble imagination can't quite make that leap. So, what conclusions have you reached?"

Before Ingrid could answer, Angelis' cell phone started to trill. She couldn't deny she was relieved at the interruption. She'd come up with no concrete theories at all. Being outsmarted by a teenage math genius wasn't a feeling she wanted to get used to.

"Sol, tell me you have some good news." As he listened to Sol Franklin's reply, Angelis' expression grew more serious.

"What's happened?" Ingrid asked him when he finally hung up.

"The end of today's session of peace negotiations has been brought forward by two hours. We now only have until ten p.m. to find her."

The taxi quickly reached the dirt track next to the field where the helicopter was waiting for them. As soon as the pilot saw them arrive, the rotor blades started up. Angelis shoved a handful of bank notes at the driver and jumped out of the cab. This time he made no attempt to open Ingrid's door.

At least he was learning.

The downdraft from the helicopter chilled Ingrid to the bone. She was used to sub zero temperatures back home—you don't get raised on a Minnesota hog farm without enduring a little discomfort come wintertime—but somehow this cold seemed to penetrate deeper. Maybe she was getting soft. Too many years in an air conditioned environment with a steady ambient temperature of seventy-two degrees could do that to an agent.

The pilot handed them each a pair of large green headphones and, once Ingrid and Angelis had clamped them onto their ears, he ordered them to buckle up. "This weather is filthy. It's coming in from the North Sea, so I'm hoping we can outrun it. But be prepared for a bumpier ride than on the way out."

When they'd reached their cruising altitude, Ingrid noticed Angelis finally release his grip from the sides of his seat. His knuckles were not so much white as translucent. "You OK?" she asked him.

"Me? Never better."

"Good—let's get back to…" She glanced toward the pilot. Whatever they said to one another, he'd be able to hear too. She made sure not to use any names. "Let's get back to the matter in hand. Maybe we're approaching this from the wrong direction."

"What do you suggest?"

"We need to try to work out what has brought her here. If not a fellow math genius, then what? Or rather, who?"

"You think she's planned a romantic liaison?"

"Hey, I know you've got great art galleries and theaters in London, but I don't think they'd be enough of a draw for her to plan something as meticulously as this. I think she's here to meet somebody."

"We're screwed then." Angelis said. "When it comes to acts of love, people behave completely irrationally."

"Love?"

"Come on, it might be difficult for you, but try to cast your mind back to when you first fell for your chap. What's his name?"

"Who?"

"Good god—your fiancé—who else?"

It took Ingrid a moment to summon an image of Marshall Claybourne in a full charm offensive. It had certainly been a while. When they'd first gotten together, Ingrid's fiancé had wooed her with his unending devotion and tireless attempts to do sweet little things for her that might make her happy. But for the last year or so, ever since he proposed, in fact, they'd been so wrapped up with work they barely even noticed one another. "How do you know about Marshall?"

"I have studied your personnel file in detail." He flashed a smile at her. "Wouldn't you have crossed rivers and scaled mountains just to be with your chap and to hell with the rest of the world?"

She frowned at him.

"Don't tell me you're immune to Cupid's arrow."

"Just make your goddamn point."

"We can't hope to preempt anything she does. We've got no chance."

"She's been pretty methodical about things up till now. I don't see any reason why she'd stop."

"Good grief, where's your sense of romance?"

The helicopter suddenly dropped forty feet without warning. The straps across Ingrid's shoulders dug hard into her flesh.

"Sorry folks," the pilot said. "You can't say I didn't warn you. I think the storm might just have caught up with us."

Angelis' face drained of color. He looked like a man who might start regretting his three course lunch.

"Hang on in there, buddy," Ingrid said, surprising herself with her sympathetic tone.

"I think that's the kindest you've been to me all day. If I'd known the threat of projectile vomiting would get that kind of response, I might have shoved a finger down my throat."

"Don't get used to it. Sympathy can wear off pretty damn fast."

"OK—for the sake of argument—let's say she's here for some romantic encounter, but let's also assume she's not so head-over-heels in love that she's lost all sense of perspective. What could she have planned?"

"Tell me more about her background."

Angelis handed Ingrid his cell phone. "All the files are on there. Read them for yourself."

"In this turbulence? It'll make me throw up faster than anything. Give me a precis."

"OK." Angelis shoved the phone back in his pocket and closed his eyes as the helicopter dropped another dozen or so feet straight down. "She went to the best school her grandmother's money could buy. She had ballet, skiing and riding lessons. And, reading between the lines, more freedom to experiment with sex and drugs than any teenager could dream of. I don't know why she's so angry at her parents. They pretty much let her do what she wanted."

"Maybe she was craving something else—like discipline and boundaries. Maybe she's angry at her parents for not providing the structure she needed."

"Craving structure and discipline? God help your kids when you have them."

"But what if she wanted to use this trip, in part, to get back at her parents? To piss them off in some way? What might she get up to that would piss them off? Or what kind of person might she be seeing that would upset them the most?" Ingrid thought about it for a moment then quickly rattled through a list of unsuitable boyfriends. But she and Angelis quickly rejected them all: Rachel Whitticker's parents would probably have welcomed anybody into their home, regardless of race, religion or gender.

The pilot's voice crackled through their headphones again. "You might want to check your seat belts are secure," he told them. "Maybe grip something tight too. It might make you feel a bit safer."

"I guess this is like a stroll in the park for you, huh?" Ingrid asked him, the edge of panic in his voice alarming her a little.

The helicopter lurched sideways, as if it were a tiny bug that had been swatted by an angry giant.

"Oh, not so much," the pilot replied. "Just got back from three years in the Gulf states. Don't get this kind of weather there. Just the odd sandstorm. And we don't fly anywhere near those things."

Angelis gulped so noisily, the pilot must have heard him.

"Don't worry though. I've practiced in a simulator." He sniffed. "Although it's never quite the same in reality."

Ingrid glanced at Angelis. His eyes were shut tight. She tried to peer through the pilot's windshield, but all she could see was gray rain. Visibility had to be down to twenty or so feet.

Though her stomach was turning cartwheels, and saliva was gathering beneath her tongue, Ingrid couldn't help feeling a slight buzz. She hadn't had this much adrenalin coursing through her veins since her very first drugs bust.

FIFTEEN

Nick Angelis' motorcycle was waiting for them when they touched back down at the heliport in Battersea. Because of the weather, the trip back from Essex took twenty minutes longer than on the way out.

They were running out of time.

"Where to now?" Angelis asked her.

"Call your company—find out if they've come up with any new leads."

"They'd call me if they had even a crumb of intel that may prove useful." He checked his phone. "No missed calls. No text messages."

It was a quarter before five. The sky was dark and the December chill was intensifying. Ingrid felt it was up to her to take control. Neither Nick Angelis nor his company had helped track down the missing teenager one little bit. She seriously doubted Angelis' claim that

Fortnum's intel was second only to Mossad's. She hoped to hell that the CIA and MI5 wouldn't have been outsmarted by a resourceful eighteen year old. "You're certain Rachel Whitticker has never been to the UK before?"

"Positive."

"But her grandmother has, presumably, plenty of times."

"Sure."

"Where does she stay during her visits?"

Angelis put in another call to his company. He hung up after less than a minute. "Whenever she visits London, she stays at the Paramount on The Strand."

"Why don't we head there?"

"Based on what?"

"The girl looks up to her grandmother, doesn't she? Respects her choices, her tastes maybe?"

"We believe that's the case."

"So maybe she'd want to stay at the same hotel."

"Do you know what a room costs at the Paramount?"

Ingrid had no clue.

"It would have completely blown her budget."

"How long to get there on the bike?"

"With a following wind, fifteen minutes."

Given how much time they'd already squandered, Ingrid decided another half hour out of their day was worth the gamble. "Let's get going then."

After running a dozen or so red lights and performing so many illegal maneuvers that at times Ingrid was forced to close her eyes, Angelis parked the bike on the sidewalk right outside the Paramount

Hotel. The liveried doorman approached them, his arm raised, his brow furrowed and his mouth open. But one withering look from Angelis stopped him in his tracks.

"We'll get this valet-parked for you, sir."

Angelis pressed a five pound note into the man's hand.

They hurried through the revolving doors and stepped into another world. Ingrid was overwhelmed by a landscape of black and white marble, colored glass light fittings suspended on thick metal chains from the ceiling, and an array of oil paintings hanging on the mahogany paneled walls. Angelis grabbed her arm and led her to the reception desk. A perfectly groomed middle-aged man smiled up at them both. His smile quickly disappeared as soon as Ingrid flashed her badge at him.

"We're looking for a missing person," she explained. "An eighteen-year-old girl who we believe may have checked in here this morning."

The receptionist frowned at her. "FBI? Do you have any jurisdiction here?"

Great, Ingrid thought, a wise-ass.

"Check with the American embassy, if you like." Ingrid handed him a card she'd been given by Sol Franklin. "An American citizen is missing and it's my job to find her."

"If you'll excuse me one moment, madam." The man turned away and made a phone call. He hung up and invited Ingrid and Angelis to take a seat.

"We're very happy to stand."

"The manager will be with you shortly."

Ingrid glanced around the front hall. A smooth-faced bell hop was hovering next to a grand brass elevator. He made eye contact with her. She nudged Angelis on the arm and said under her breath, "Keep the receptionist busy."

Angelis leaned on the low desk, instantly obscuring the receptionist's view of Ingrid and the elevator.

Ingrid wandered over to the bell hop. "Hi. I wonder if you can help me. I'm looking for someone who I think could be in a little trouble. She would have checked in earlier today. She's very young, long brown hair, real pretty, slim. Did you see her?"

"Might have. What's it worth to you?"

Ingrid pulled her wallet from her purse and plucked out three twenty pound notes. It was all the cash she had. She handed it to the young bell hop, who deftly slipped it into a pocket. Ingrid glanced over her shoulder—Angelis was still shielding her from the attentions of the receptionist.

"Do you know which room she's in?"

"Carried her bag there myself."

"She had a bag?"

"Just a little backpack."

"Which room?"

The bell hop swiped a credit card sized rectangle of plastic along a sensor beneath the elevator up and down buttons. The elevator doors opened. "Level four, room 443. Turn left out of the lift." He passed her the plastic card. "This'll get you in. Be sure to bring it back to me."

Before she disappeared inside the elevator, Ingrid glanced once again in Angelis' direction. He was still occupied at the reception desk.

The doors pinged open on level four and Ingrid found herself stepping onto thick, deep pile carpet. She headed left, down a corridor that was decorated with fine silk-woven wallpaper. It really was another world. She followed the numbered signs and quickly reached room 443. She leaned in toward the door and listened. There were no sounds coming from inside. She didn't see how announcing her presence would help any, so she slipped the key card into the lock and levered down the handle. The door clicked open. Ingrid took a deep breath and pushed it wide.

The main room was empty.

Closing the door quietly behind her, she stepped inside. There was an interior door to her left. The bathroom, she supposed. Again she leaned in close and listened. The low burbling of running water filtered through the door. Ingrid tested the handle. The door opened without resistance. She pushed through the doorway, expecting to see a figure inside a steamy shower cubicle. Instead, she discovered water gushing from the mixer faucet into the unplugged drain of an empty bathtub. She spun around 360 degrees. The bathroom was empty. Opposite the door, something caught Ingrid's eye. Written on the mirror above the sink in bright pink lipstick, were the words: *nice try, but too late.* A large pink 'X' filled the remainder of the space.

SIXTEEN

Ingrid made a quick search of the room. The closet was empty, as were the safe and mini refrigerator. Apart from the scrawled message in the bathroom, no sign of Rachel Whitticker remained.

They'd been out maneuvered by a precocious teenager once again and Ingrid was starting to feel decidedly dumb.

Goddammit, there had to be some way of turning things around.

She returned to the grand reception hall via the bell hop and handed him back the key card.

"Find what you were looking for?" he asked her.

"Not quite."

"If there's anything else I can do…"

"I don't think that'll be necessary."

She marched back to the reception desk to find Angelis arguing with a gray haired man dressed in a suit that wouldn't have looked out of place at a wedding.

"We have to protect the privacy of our guests. I'm sure you understand that," she heard him tell Angelis in an unmistakable and no doubt well rehearsed supercilious tone.

When Angelis spotted her, he turned away from the desk while the manager was still in full flow. "Well?"

"We were on the right tracks. Just one or two hours too late."

He followed her back out onto the street. "She was here?"

Ingrid told him about the message Rachel had left them.

"Cheeky bloody minx." He shook his head. "Although I can't help admiring her style." He looked around for the doorman.

The motorcycle arrived a couple of minutes later.

"We're no nearer finding her," Ingrid said as Angelis handed her a helmet. "I'm beginning to think I've been missing something really obvious."

"We have some of the finest brains in the intelligence service working on this case."

"Maybe you should put them through an IQ test. Math genius Rachel Whitticker is making us all look stupid." Ingrid pushed her short hair off her forehead and tucked it into the helmet, but kept the visor up. "I just feel I need go back to law enforcement basics."

"Which are?"

"First thing is to put yourself in the shoes of the perpetrator."

"She hasn't actually committed any crime."

"You know what I mean." Ingrid climbed onto the bike ahead of Angelis. "You certainly can't describe her as a victim." She ran a hand along the handlebars.

"Want to take her for a spin?"

Her mouth dropped open. "You bet. Just as long as you make sure you grab the back of the seat and not my ass when we turn corners."

"When have I behaved in anything less than a gentlemanly manner?"

Ingrid thought about it for a moment. It was true. Angelis acted the part of a smooth operator, but he hadn't actually made any moves on her. For which she was immensely grateful.

"I'll give you directions," Angelis told her.

"Where are we headed?"

"Back to the embassy." Angelis swung his right leg over the bike. He settled himself on the rear of the seat. "So tell me, what theories have you come up with, putting yourself in her shoes?"

"She's planned this whole thing quite carefully. She came to the UK today. Not yesterday, or the day before. I think she's definitely here for a specific event."

"And there's some sort of romantic liaison involved?"

"Uh huh—with someone that'll piss off her parents."

Angelis pulled a face.

"You don't like my theory?"

"I want to, I really do, but isn't it all a tad far-fetched? What if her grandmother had refused to bring her to Europe?"

"From what we know about her, it seems Rachel Whitticker has the Secretary of State wrapped around her little finger." Before Angelis had time to consider his response, Ingrid started the engine and accelerated into a gap in the traffic.

*

Sol Franklin was waiting for them in the underground parking lot when they arrived. "The administration clerk in the Criminal Investigation Unit is at your disposal," he told them as soon as Ingrid had switched off the engine. "She's great at digging up information. They invented the phrase 'dogged determination' with Jennifer in mind."

"I thought we couldn't risk accessing the Bureau's files, in case it raised an alarm," Ingrid said.

"Given the time constraints, we may be past worrying about that. Besides, I'm sure we can be creative with our digging."

"That's great. There are a couple of angles I'd like to pursue."

"There are?" Angelis raised his eyebrows.

"I still need to get under Rachel's skin a little to work out what she's planning."

"If you think that'll help." Sol Franklin didn't sound at all convinced. Ingrid decided to change the subject.

"Any update on the expected end time of today's negotiation session?"

"We're still working on twenty-two hundred hours." He looked at his watch. "You have less than four and a half hours to save the day."

Sol led them up to the third floor and into a low-ceilinged office, about twenty feet by thirty. There were three desks: two backed up against one another on one side of the room, the third, slightly larger than the other two, stood on its own pushed up against the opposite wall. Sitting at one of the paired desks was a slightly heavy, sandy-haired woman in her early twenties. Sol strode toward her, told her not to get up, and introduced Ingrid. It seemed the woman already knew Angelis. In fact, her cheeks started to flush as soon as he approached her: the many freckles on her face merging into an pinkish-brown blush.

"As ever, a pleasure, Jennifer." Angelis treated her to a roguish smile.

The clerk giggled like a school girl and dipped her chin in faux bashfulness.

Ingrid glanced at the two empty desks. "All on your own?" she asked the clerk.

Jennifer nodded, then glanced at Sol. He gave her an almost imperceptible nod before she started speaking. "There's another clerk, who sits right here next to me, but he has a day off today." Her accent was pure southern California.

"And this desk?"

Again Jennifer sought Sol Franklin's approval before speaking. That's… I mean… that *was* Agent

Mulroony's desk. He… ah… he doesn't work here anymore."

Another reassuring nod from Franklin.

"Has Sol told you about the girl we're looking for?" Ingrid asked.

"Spoiled brat who also happens to be a genius. Fights all the time with her parents but is her grandmother's favorite."

"Yep—that pretty well sums up everything I know about her." She smiled at Jennifer. "I've been thinking about her relationship with her parents. If we assume Rachel sees herself as a rebel and the people she most wants to rebel against are her parents, then maybe we need to work out exactly what would piss them off the most."

"Running away to Europe aged eighteen would have freaked my parents out. They weren't too happy when I did it aged twenty-two! Even though I was working for the government."

"Their loss is our gain." Angelis winked at her.

Jennifer flushed in an instant.

"We're currently working on the assumption that Rachel's here for some kind of special event and to meet somebody—"

"And that somebody is a man?" Jennifer interrupted, doing her best not to look at Angelis.

"For the sake of argument, let's assume that too," Ingrid said, "I've been giving it some serious thought and I've come to the conclusion that there's only one kind of individual Rachel could date that would really piss off her mom and dad."

Angelis shrugged at her. Sol Franklin did the same.

"A Republican." Ingrid wasn't at all sure her theory was strong enough to stand much scrutiny, but she braced herself for a barrage of doubting questions. They didn't come.

"Her parents were huge fundraisers for both Obama campaigns," Sol Franklin said. "If she were to date a Republican, it would certainly embarrass them."

"My God, it actually seems blindingly obvious now you've mentioned it." Angelis beamed at her. "I think you might be on to something."

"So we're looking for a Republican right here in London?" Jennifer's fingers were poised over her keyboard.

"Who presumably moved to London fairly recently," Ingrid said.

"How so?" Sol Franklin was leaning over the desk.

"I'm supposing Rachel met him in the US. I can't imagine her having the patience to deal with a long distance relationship for very long. It can't have been going on long enough for her to get bored."

Sol Franklin checked his watch. "Listen, I've got to go. I have a meeting with the chief. You keep me posted."

They waved their goodbyes.

"So… we need a Republican in London," Ingrid said. "How many can there be?"

Jennifer turned toward her computer and started to type rapidly. "Should I check for senators and congressmen who are visiting at the moment?"

"I doubt it would be anyone that high profile," Ingrid said. She wondered how she could make such pronouncements when in reality she didn't have much more of a clue than either Jennifer or Angelis. But somehow she felt the longer the search went on, the more it was her responsibility to find Rachel, having gotten so close at the hotel.

"Not that high profile or that old," Angelis added. "Unless Rachel has some father figure fixation. Given how she feels about her own dad, I would imagine that's not the case."

"OK—just look for anyone under thirty." Ingrid looked at the clerk's computer screen over her shoulder. "They'd have to have some kind of reputation, be notable in political circles at least—otherwise the relationship just wouldn't have the same impact on Rachel's parents.

"Then why don't I check all Republican members of both houses—and major fund raisers for the party—and see if any of them have sons who are the right age? Then we'll find out if any of them are working or studying in the UK."

"You're bloody brilliant!" Angelis said and pecked Jennifer on the top of her head.

The clerk blushed again, this time more vividly than she had before. "You may want to sit down. It could take a while."

Ingrid looked at her watch. "Fine, just make sure you're no longer than twenty minutes."

SEVENTEEN

"How's it going?" Ingrid asked Jennifer at the nineteen minute mark. The clerk had made it clear she didn't want to be scrutinized as she worked, so Ingrid had been relegated to former Agent Mulroony's desk. The first thing she'd done when she'd sat down was rummage through the drawers beneath the desk, eager to keep her hands occupied, if not her mind. All the drawers were empty. Not even a pencil or an eraser remained. The guy must have taken every last item of stationery with him when he left.

"I have a list of eligible Republican sons and another list of work permits and student visas issued to US citizens in the last six months. Now I just need to cross reference the two lists," Jennifer announced.

"Won't that take forever?"Ingrid asked.

"Not if I input the data into one of my spreadsheets." Jennifer tapped the 'enter' key and sat back. "There. No time at all. We have…" She peered a little more closely at the screen. "Fifteen possible candidates."

"That many?"

"London is a very popular destination for internships."

Nick Angelis was sitting at the desk opposite Jennifer with his feet up. "Tracking fifteen potential suitors might be a stretch before ten p.m. Depending on where they all are."

"Maybe we can rule some of them out quite quickly." Ingrid returned to her earlier position standing behind the clerk's chair. She didn't give a damn how off-putting it was. This was officially her mission, after all. She stabbed a finger toward the screen. "How about this guy at the top of the list?"

Jennifer swiveled in her chair to a second computer—a laptop shoved to the corner of her desk. Her fingers moved swiftly over the keys. "Dougie Richards," she read from the screen, "twenty-four years old. Here working for a media company in Soho." She switched back to the first screen. "His dad's a congressman. Very friendly with the anti gun control lobby."

Angelis dragged his feet from the desk and sat up. "Sounds promising. Do you have an address for him?"

Jennifer switched machines again. "Oh drat," she said. "That's no good at all." She smiled apologetically at Angelis. "According to the database, he's gay."

"That's not bad news at all—we are trying to rule people out. Good work, Jen."

Jennifer beamed at him.

"Carry on at this rate and we'll get through the whole list before teatime."

"I'm sorry, I should have asked. Can I get you a tea? Or a coffee?"

"No—I wasn't hinting. Who's next?"

The clerk squinted at the screen. Ingrid wondered if maybe Jennifer needed glasses but didn't like to wear them when Nick Angelis was around. "OK—next up it's Ray Donaldson." She swiveled in her seat a few times as she checked both computers. "He should stay on the list. He's the right age, his mom's a senator and he's currently working in a high profile ad agency. The company he works for makes all the advertisements for the Conservative Party." She looked over her shoulder at Ingrid. "They're like the Republicans back home, only better educated."

"Thanks for explaining that for me," Ingrid said, deciding to let the patronizing tone of the clerk's voice wash right over her. Now wasn't the time for her to prove she wasn't an ill-informed farm girl from the Midwest. "Who's next?"

"This guy's mom raised funds in Alaska a fews ago. She's a fierce Tea Party supporter. Now she's got political ambitions of her own."

"And what about him? Is he a suitable candidate?"

Jennifer switched to the laptop. "Ah… not so much. He's here with his pregnant nineteen-year-old bride."

"Is it possible he's cheating on her?" Angelis asked.

"Not judging by the speech his mom gave recently about the sanctity of family. The scandal would ruin her campaign before it even got started."

They went through another four names on the list and managed to eliminate three of them.

"How many do we have left as potentials?" Ingrid peered at the tiny font on Jennifer's spreadsheet.

"Ten in total, but there are still eight more to look at."

"This is taking too long." Ingrid turned to Angelis. "Can't we recruit your data guys and speed things up a little?"

"How do you propose we do that?"

"Jennifer—do you have photographs of all the remaining possible candidates?"

"Passport pictures of them. Pretty good quality."

"How about we send them to Fortnum's and they can maybe cross match with the pictures uploaded to Rachel Whitticker's social media platforms?"

"Rachel's been covering her tracks very carefully—it's unlikely there'd be a photograph of him," Angelis said.

"Maybe she's not as perfect as we're giving her credit for. It's just possible she made a mistake, isn't it?"

Angelis shrugged back at her, but nevertheless gave Jennifer the email address of one of the tech guys at Fortnum's headquarters. "I suppose it can't do any harm."

"OK," Ingrid said, staring at the spreadsheet once again, "what about this next guy?"

"No—unless you think Rachel's some place other than London. He's doing a PhD at Edinburgh University."

"Strike him off the list. Anyone else studying or working outside of the capital?"

The clerk switched between machines again. "Two others—one in Exeter, the other in Cambridge."

Angelis shot Ingrid a glance.

"You're certain Rachel's in London?" Jennifer asked.

"We've had to make educated guesses all day," Ingrid replied, sensing using the word 'educated' was a little misleading. 'Wild stabs in the dark' would be closer to the truth. "Leave the Cambridge guy on the list for now."

"Just a handful more to look at."

"Out of those remaining, whose family is the most right wing?"

"I'm not sure I can make that judgment." Jennifer looked to Angelis for support.

"It is a rather subjective decision to make about them," he said.

"OK—how about a checklist? They should be: anti-choice, anti-gun control, pro small government, pro big corporation tax breaks, global warming skeptics…" Ingrid suddenly ran out of steam. She'd based her list on all the policies her mother supported. She wasn't sure where her mom stood on economic protectionism.

"OK. I get the picture. Give me a couple of minutes."

"Sure." Ingrid started to pace up and down.

"You think Rachel really wants to go all out to embarrass her parents?" Angelis was tapping his cell phone against his dark stubbly chin as he spoke.

"We've got to try something to get the list down. We've pretty much run out of time."

Jennifer swiveled in her chair to face them just as Angelis' phone started to buzz against his dimpled chin.

"We're down to two—the guy in Cambridge and another one right here in London," the clerk told them.

Angelis answered his phone, spent a matter of seconds listening to the person on the other end and hung up. "Is one of them called Eugene Barclay, by any chance?"

"Your tech guys found a match on the photographs?" Ingrid asked, sounding more incredulous than she'd meant.

"Seems Mr Barclay added a profile picture—against the express wishes of Rachel Whitticker, one suspects."

"Maybe he did it recently."

Jennifer brought up Barclay's details on her screen. "Oh my gosh," she said. "He's working as an assistant for a Conservative MP named Hugh Hollingsworth."

"An MP? Does that mean he's in Westminster?"

Jennifer nodded at Ingrid.

"Westminster's quite close, isn't it?" Ingrid said, pleased she could demonstrate the little she knew of London geography.

"It certainly is," Angelis said, "we can be there in less than ten minutes."

EIGHTEEN

Jennifer found the address for the MP's office. Ingrid was a little disappointed to discover it wasn't within the Houses of Parliament, but some building on the other side of the street. Sol Franklin called ahead to ensure Ingrid and Angelis would be able to get past the front desk, but was careful not to divulge the nature of their visit.

Just as Angelis had promised, the motorcycle ride took under ten minutes. He parked the bike on Victoria Embankment, the street that ran alongside the Thames between Blackfriars and Westminster Bridges—in an attempt to improve her knowledge of London, Ingrid had checked the map on her phone before they left the embassy—and they ran from the street to the reception lobby of Portcullis House.

As soon as they were through the doors, they were confronted with a metal detector, a bag search desk and two security officers who looked like they should have been playing quarterback for the New York Giants. Angelis waved one of them toward him, whispered something gently into his ear, and showed him an ID badge. The big man clapped a meaty paw on Angelis' shoulder and started to guide him toward the reception desk. Angelis pulled up and pointed toward Ingrid. The security guard nodded and put a guiding hand around her waist, somehow managing to touch her so lightly, she didn't have to resist the urge to push away his arm.

Angelis checked in with the uniformed woman behind the desk and was told to take a seat. "We are in rather a hurry. Any chance we could go straight up?"

"Ms Tipton will be down presently," the woman said firmly.

"Who?"

"Sir Hugh Hollingsworth's personal secretary."

Ingrid looked at Angelis. She pulled him away from the desk. "I thought our guy was the MP's secretary."

"Assistant. Probably research assistant. Though I've never been entirely clear exactly what it is they find to research. An excuse to claim more expenses, I suppose. It's also possible Barclay's paying handsomely for the opportunity to work with a senior UK politician."

"Paying Hollingsworth?"

"One of the perks of the job." He checked the time. "Let's give it a few minutes. If this Tipton woman doesn't arrive swiftly, we'll just have to—"

"Hello? Mr Angelis?" A woman emerged from an elevator on the other side of the lobby. "I'm afraid Sir Hugh is very busy. He asked me to extend his apologies—"

Angelis put up a hand to stop her. He smiled and strode over to the elevator, his arm extended. He shook her hand in both of his. "Thank you so much for seeing us so promptly. This is Ingrid Skyberg—from the American embassy."

Ingrid nodded a hello as she joined them. "Actually, we'd really like to speak to Sir Hugh's research assistant—Eugene Barclay?" she said.

The secretary seemed to grimace slightly at the mention of his name. "Eugene left at lunchtime. He won't be in for the rest of the day."

"Really? Where is he?" Ingrid asked.

"I've absolutely no idea."

Ingrid flashed a look at Angelis, who quickly pulled his cell phone from a pocket. "I'm on it," he said.

While Angelis called his company to have a surveillance team sent to Barclay's house, Ingrid pulled Ms Tipton gently to one side. "In that case, I think a chat with Sir Hugh is absolutely essential."

"I told you—he has a completely full diary."

Ingrid lowered her voice. "I'd hate to have to escalate matters with the Foreign Office. Diplomatic channels can get so bureaucratic, don't you find? Endless questions to answer. Disruption for the MP, more work for his staff." Ingrid prayed she'd chosen the correct government department to threaten the woman with.

The secretary narrowed her eyes, staring into Ingrid's face longer than was entirely comfortable. "I can give you five minutes with him. But that's it. Sir Hugh shouldn't even be here. If it wasn't for the fundraiser this evening, he would already have left for his constituency."

"Five minutes should be plenty."

As they followed Ms Tipton to the elevator, Angelis said in hushed tones, "We've got four men checking out Barclay's place. They should be there in less than fifteen minutes."

"What if he's not there?"

"Let's throw ourselves off that bridge when we come to it, shall we?"

Once they'd stepped out of the elevator on the fourth floor, Ms Tipton led them down a wide, well-lit corridor and into an outer room containing one large desk and one small, the small one pushed against the wall on the far side. It was empty except for a computer monitor. File cabinets ran along the length of the left hand wall. On top was a selection of lush green plants in ceramic pots.

"Wait here for a moment, would you?" The secretary hurried to an inner door and knocked sharply. She disappeared inside and reemerged just a few seconds later. "Sir Hugh will see you now. Five minutes. No longer."

"Thank you, ma'am." Ingrid's warm smile wasn't returned.

They followed Tipton into the inner office to find a middle-aged, flabby, floppy-haired blond man sitting behind his desk, speaking on his cell phone. "I'll call you back later, darling" he mumbled into the phone and hung up.

Angelis stepped forward and introduced them both. The fat MP stared at Ingrid.

"The American embassy, eh? International incident is it?"

"I'm sorry, sir?" Ingrid said.

"Veronica here seems to think the Foreign Office is involved." He looked up at his secretary who had taken up a defensive position behind his desk.

"Not at this point, Sir Hugh," Angelis said. "That's what we're trying to avoid."

The MP patted Tipton on the behind. "Really Veronica, you must tame that overactive imagination of yours." His hand lingered. His secretary didn't quite manage to control the shudder that rippled across her shoulders as she stepped away from his grasp.

Right away, Ingrid's attitude to the hostile woman softened. She shouldn't have to endure that kind of behavior. Which century was Hollingsworth living in?

"So if not an international crisis—what is it?" the MP asked.

"We'd like to speak to your assistant, Eugene Barclay. Where can we find him?" Ingrid asked.

"God knows."

"Sir?"

"I gave him the afternoon off. His young lady is visiting from America."

"You've met her?" Ingrid struggled to keep the excitement from her voice.

"I've not had the pleasure. But the lovesick fool couldn't stop talking about her. Driving you mad, wasn't he, Veronica?"

The secretary said nothing.

"What is this all about?" Hollingsworth shoved his flamboyant blond bangs out of his eyes. "Eugene came highly recommended. Good upstanding Southern family—perhaps a little too Tea Party for my own tastes, but a genuinely decent chap."

"Do you know if his girlfriend is staying with him at his apartment?" Ingrid directed her question squarely at Ms Tipton. If Barclay had been so eager to talk about his new love interest, Tipton would be the one with the vital information.

The secretary glanced at her boss, reluctant to answer.

"Why on earth do you want to know a thing like that?" Hollingsworth said. "Unless you tell me exactly what this is about, I'm afraid I'll have to ask you to leave."

"We believe the girl he's seeing is missing from home. She's a US citizen and we need to speak to her urgently."

"Why is the FBI involved?"

"It's standard procedure in the circumstances," Angelis said.

"And I'm still not clear exactly what your role is in all this." Hollingsworth narrowed his eyes and stared up at Angelis through the thick locks of blond hair that had fallen back across his forehead.

"Advice and support."

"And has this young woman actually done anything wrong?"

"She's missing from home."

"Are you even certain Eugene's girlfriend is the girl you're looking for?"

"We have a pretty good idea," Ingrid said, unable to be more categoric, given the false trails Rachel had already left.

"I'm not sure that's good enough. You have no jurisdiction here. I'm beginning to come around to Eugene's point of view. Perhaps small government does make sense." He leaned back in his chair. "It seems to me neither Eugene nor his young lady have committed any crime. Why not let these two young lovebirds have a little time together?"

"Don't you want to help reunite a family with their missing daughter?" Ingrid couldn't understand why Hollingsworth had decided to be so obstructive. Maybe it had something to do with how much he was getting paid to have Barclay as his assistant.

"How old is she?"

"Eighteen."

"Quite old enough to know her own mind." Hollingsworth stood up. His shirt was half hanging out of his pants, his large belly spilling over his waistband. "Now, if you don't mind, I have rather a busy schedule. Veronica will show you out."

The secretary made sure she didn't walk past her boss as she slipped around the desk and strode toward the door. She escorted them into the elevator. As she pressed the lobby button, she smoothed down her crumpled skirt.

Ingrid edged a little closer to her. "I had a boss like that once."

Ms Tipton didn't respond.

"It wasn't until five of us lodged official complaints that anything was actually done. I guess it'd be difficult for that to happen here."

Tipton continued to hold her tongue.

The elevator doors opened and as Ingrid and Angelis stepped out into the foyer, the secretary wished them luck in finding the missing girl. The doors closed again before Ingrid had a chance to respond. They got as far as the reception desk when Angelis' phone started to ring. He answered quickly, listened intently for a few seconds, then hung up.

"No sign of anyone at Barclay's flat. The team will stay there, just in case he tips up later. He's switched off his mobile phone too."

"Dammit. There has to be something we can do."

"Frankly, I'm all out of ideas."

Just as they started to head for the exit, Ingrid heard someone call her name from the other side of the foyer. She turned to discover Ms Tipton standing next to the elevator. Ingrid hurried over to her.

"Eugene is going to the fundraiser this evening," she told Ingrid in a whisper. "He asked me to get a ticket for his girlfriend."

Angelis joined them.

"Can you give me the details?" Ingrid retrieved her phone from her purse, ready to punch in the address and time of the event.

In the same quiet voice, Ms Tipton provided the information. Once Ingrid had returned her phone to her purse, the secretary said, "I am doing something, by the way. About my… situation. He's not going to get away with it for much longer." She raised her eyes toward the ceiling.

"I'm very glad to hear that."

"Thanks for your concern." With that, the elevator doors opened and Tipton slipped inside.

Angelis checked his watch. "My God we're going to be cutting it fine."

"I'm sorry?"

"We've got to get you kitted out in a ball gown."

"What?"

Angelis stopped walking and turned to her, he took a little bow. "Would you do me the honor of accompanying me to the ball?"

NINETEEN

Ingrid wriggled uncomfortably in the silk upholstered chair of a private suite in Harvey Nichols department store. She was wearing a toweling bath robe over her underwear and felt horribly exposed. She silently cursed Sol Franklin for agreeing to Angelis' stupid scheme to lift Rachel Whitticker straight out of the fundraising ball.

"It makes a lot of sense," Sol had said. "We can keep an eye on her movements up close and you and Nick can blend right in as the best looking couple at the ball. Plus you'll be able to choose exactly the right moment to apprehend her. No fuss, no mess." He'd sounded as if Angelis had written his script for him.

Ingrid was beginning to think they'd ganged up against her.

After a hurried discussion, it had been agreed between the three of them that, in order to keep the whole incident from the Secretary of State, they should locate the girl, reunite her with the original French bodyguard and concoct some tale about a day trip to London that lasted much longer than Rachel had planned. That way hopefully no one at the embassy in Paris would be blamed for the incompetence of the French security company and Rachel wouldn't fall out with her grandmother. But they had very little time to pull it all off. Especially if Rachel Whitticker didn't agree to the scheme. If the girl put up any resistance, then the plan was pretty much dead in the water.

"Miss Skyberg, thank you for your patience." The heavily made-up assistant with the bleached blond hair appeared at the fitting room door with three full-length dresses over her arm.

They all looked hideous.

Ingrid wanted to scream at her—it wasn't *Miss* Skyberg, it was *Agent* Skyberg—and she was feeling anything but patient.

"Your husband not around to give you a second opinion?"

"He's not my husband."

"Oh I'm sorry. It's just that you seemed so well suited, I presumed you'd tied the knot already."

Ingrid had to stop herself grimacing at the suggestion. She glanced at the dresses and actually felt a little nauseous. She hated shopping for clothes. She hated shopping, period. In her opinion, if something couldn't be easily ordered online, it wasn't worth having.

"I've got these three and I've identified half a dozen others, if these ones don't suit."

Ingrid had already tried on and rejected four dresses. She was tempted to just grab the first dress from the assistant's arm and tell her she'd take it. But she still had a little pride in her appearance. She didn't want to end up looking like a clown. The assistant hung up the dresses in the fitting room and stepped outside.

"Just ring the bell here when you're in the first one and need a bit of help with the zip."

Ingrid reluctantly got to her feet and selected the least worse option of the three. It was black and backless, but mercifully had no sparkling fake diamonds stitched onto it. It also had shoulder straps—at least she wouldn't feel as if she were permanently slipping out of it. She closed the the fitting room door, took off the robe and stepped into the dress, unable at first to even glance at the 360 degree mirrors. She took a deep breath and raised her gaze. She exhaled. It really didn't look that bad. But there was no way to judge it properly from this distance. She reached up and yanked open the door and immediately wished she hadn't.

Nick Angelis was sitting on a silk covered chair right outside. He smiled slyly at her. "My word, Agent Skyberg, you do scrub up well. You look like a fairytale princess."

"Screw you, Angelis."

"Until, of course, you open your mouth." He stood up. "Stop the search," he said, turning to the assistant.

"We have found the perfect dress. All we need now are shoes, hair and makeup."

Right on cue, a woman with a flawless, perfectly matte complexion appeared at the outer door, armed with a plastic transparent toolbox of cosmetics.

"Are you sure about this?" Ingrid asked Angelis.

"Absolutely—this one sets off your curves in all the right places."

"I wasn't talking about the dress, goddammit!"

"No?"

"What if this whole fundraising ball is just another false trail that she's left us? What if we're doing exactly what she wants us to be doing? Meanwhile she and her Republican boyfriend are laughing at the stupid government employees."

The makeup woman and shopping assistant threw each other a puzzled glance.

"Just discussing work," Angelis said by way of explanation.

"You work together?" the assistant said. "How lovely is that? You must really get on well with one another. If I spend more than a couple of hours with my other half we're at each other's throats. Holidays are a complete nightmare."

"We work together, period," Ingrid clarified. "He's not my husband, or my boyfriend… or even my friend."

Angelis' face took on an exaggerated hurt look. "She can be so cruel sometimes. But it doesn't stop me hoping she'll come around one day."

"Ahhhh," the makeup woman and assistant purred in unison.

Good grief.

Ingrid thought she might throw up. If she could have run right out of there and headed for her hotel, refusing to emerge until they found her somebody else to work with, she would have in an instant. But for what remained of this mission, she knew she was stuck with him, for better or worse. Thank God she would never have to see him again once it was over.

"You still haven't answered my question," she said.

"Veronica Tipton seemed pretty certain they'd be there."

"So she's been duped too. My God, Nick, can't you see it's possible we're being played here? Again."

He smiled at her.

"What? What did I say that's so amusing?"

"That's the first time you've used my Christian name."

"It was a mistake."

"Ouch!"

"Are we wasting time we don't have to spare going to this fundraising thing?"

"We have his flat under surveillance, the tech guys have come up with nothing new."

"But shouldn't we at least formulate a plan B, if they're not there tonight?"

"That's precisely what we don't have time for. We have to give this our best shot. It's the only game in town."

The makeup woman dumped her toolbox noisily on a nearby table and took a step closer to Ingrid. "If I don't make a start soon, you won't be going to the ball at all, Cinders."

Ingrid closed her eyes and prayed the ordeal would be over quickly.

TWENTY

Ingrid and Angelis arrived at the white stucco Georgian venue on Whitehall a little after seven-thirty. Ingrid could only hope that the operation would go smoothly. She'd called Sol Franklin from the car. He'd assured her she had his full support to apprehend the missing teenager "using reasonable force." She hadn't asked him to elucidate. If Angelis' performance with a bucket of water was anything to go by, she and Franklin had a whole different definition of the word reasonable.

The chauffeur—an embassy driver, complete with smart cap and dark gray uniform—pulled into the curb. As he started to get out of the car, Angelis stopped him and climbed out himself. He scooted around the back and yanked open her door, extending a hand. Much as Ingrid wanted to ignore it, she wasn't sure how stable she'd be on the uneven sidewalk in such high heels. She grabbed his hand and levered herself up. By the time she had straightened up, she was almost as tall as him.

"Allow me to tell you again how beautiful you look this evening, Ingrid."

"You can say it again, but I can't promise I won't throw up all over your tuxedo."

He stepped back from her, his gaze tracking down from her head to her pointed silver shoes. "Exquisite."

"For God's sake let me get inside. I'm freezing out here with no jacket." She wrapped her black silk shawl closer to her. "It's got to be below zero tonight."

Angelis held out his arm. Again, uncertain of her hold on vertical, she accepted the assistance. This operation had better succeed. Already she was feeling mildly humiliated by the experience.

"Oh bollocks and bloody bugger," Angelis suddenly exclaimed under his breath. He nodded toward the entrance of the grand building.

There was a tight scrum of photographers standing just outside. The plump man Angelis had had the altercation with that morning in Grosvenor Square—it seemed impossible that it had been the same day—was standing at the head of the pack.

"If he recognizes us and informs his reporter chum, we'll never keep this operation under wraps," Angelis said. "We should probably go into the building through the kitchen."

But it was too late. The fat photographer was pointing his long lens straight at them.

"We do look a little different than we did earlier," Ingrid said, hopefully. She couldn't face the prospect of hobbling any further in her shoes than she had to.

"He's seen us now anyway. Let's brazen it out." Angelis marched Ingrid to the entrance and straight inside without comment from the photographer. The burly man checking the invites at the door waved them through without question.

"One of your colleagues from Fortnum's?" Ingrid asked as she was glided into the warmth and bright lights of a plushly decorated lobby. It looked a little like a five-star hotel.

"Not exactly." Angelis handed the two gold-embossed invitation cards to a man in livery. "Ex-military. I served with him in Iraq.

"I never asked—how much back up do we have here tonight?"

"You think it's not something we can handle between the two of us?"

"You're telling me there's no back up?"

"Containment is key, remember. More personnel means a greater risk of the details getting out." He dragged her along the thick red carpet and through a porticoed arch into an enormous ballroom. Tables were ranged all the way around the edges of the room. Most were occupied. A handful of brave souls had taken to the dance floor. Either they were exhibitionists or they'd started drinking much earlier in the day. Ingrid glanced at some of the diners, looking out for Rachel Whitticker. Waiters were weaving between the tables, delivering the first course. Ingrid was suddenly ravenous.

"Care for a dance?" Angelis asked, his hand outstretched.

"I'll pass if it's all the same to you."

"That's not an option, I'm afraid. The only way to check all the tables without arousing suspicion is via the dance floor. So I suggest we strut our stuff."

"I can't dance."

"What?"

"Not like that."

"Just allow yourself to be led. I promise not to step on your precious feet."

Before Ingrid had a chance to object, Angelis grabbed her around the waist and dragged her into the middle of the room.

"I'll scan the tables while you distract them with your perfectly formed back."

The tempo of the music slowed suddenly as the band switched from some Latin American rhythm to a sedate waltz. Angelis didn't miss a beat. They'd made it half way around the circumference of the room when he said, "There she is, three o'clock, if the stage is midnight."

Ingrid started to crane her neck around.

"Not now! I'll turn you slowly so you can take a look."

They gracefully rotated 180 degrees. Ingrid spotted Rachel Whitticker sitting at a table, clearly embarrassing the other diners by nuzzling Eugene Barclay's neck. "If her grandmother could see her now," Ingrid said and realized she sounded just like her old high school principal.

"Thankfully the Secretary of State has been spared the spectacle," Angelis said. "The sooner we separate those two, the better." He turned Ingrid again.

"We can't exactly dance right over and snatch her."

"No." Angelis shifted his gaze from Rachel Whitticker's table momentarily and stared into Ingrid's eyes. He smiled. "Besides, I'm rather enjoying myself."

Ingrid pushed his left hand from her waist and yanked away her hand from his right. "We'll wait until she visits the restroom and I'll make my move then." She peered into her tiny silver purse. It was barely big enough for a cell phone and a credit card. Thankfully, she'd remembered to shove a lipstick in there too. She hurried off the dance floor, Angelis trailing in her wake. "Which table is ours? I feel far too conspicuous parading around like this."

Angelis scooped up her hand and led her to a table next to the exit. They sat down.

"Good location," Ingrid admitted.

"I do give these matters some consideration, you know."

Ingrid eyed the basket piled high with artisan buns and tiny slices of seeded bread. She didn't want to load up on carb, especially given the snugness of her dress, but she may not have time to wait for the first course to arrive. She poured herself a large glass of water and buttered a wholewheat bun. She sank her teeth into the bread and allowed herself a little relieved exhale. The intel Sir Hugh Hollingsworth's secretary had given them had been accurate. They hadn't been cavorting around a dance floor in fancy dress for nothing.

Thank God.

"I ordered for us in advance," Angelis said as he watched her devour the first half of the bread roll. "I went for fish, chicken and a cheese dessert, just to be on the safe side."

"Nice idea—but I don't think we'll be eating." Ingrid nodded toward Rachel Whitticker's table.

The girl was on her feet, blowing Barclay extravagant kisses as if she were about to leave the country, rather than visit the bathroom. Ingrid stood up.

"I'll wait in the corridor outside," Angelis said, and pushed back his chair.

"We can't both follow her to the ladies' restroom. She's not stupid." Ingrid studied the girl's gait for a moment. "Even though she might be a little drunk." She shook her head. "Best place for you is the front entrance, just in case I lose her."

"Shame we couldn't discreetly attach a wire to you."

"In this dress? There's barely enough space for me. I have my phone."

"You will call if you get into trouble?"

"She's an eighteen-year-old math student. I think I can handle it. You must be getting me confused with some French security guard."

The restroom was located down two flights of stairs and along a seemingly endless corridor. Ingrid stayed as far back as she dared, stopping and looking into her purse whenever she sensed Rachel Whitticker slowing down. The girl's demeanor had changed dramatically. The unsteady walk had disappeared—she held her head high and strode forward purposefully.

Ingrid figured the tipsy ingenue act was designed to appeal to Eugene Barclay. Left to her own devices, Rachel Whitticker seemed completely in control of all major motor functions.

Finally she arrived at the restroom and slipped inside. Ingrid waited a few seconds then followed her in. She was surprised to discover the brightly lit bathroom was empty. In a venue this grand she had expected an attendant waiting to hand a tiny towel to visitors after they'd washed their hands. Two of the stalls, however, were occupied. Ingrid went into the third, made sure she locked the door noisily, waited another couple of seconds, rattled the toilet tissue dispenser, and yanked the flush. From the stall next to hers there erupted an awful retching noise. It wasn't yet eight-thirty. Someone had a pretty crappy night ahead of them.

Ingrid slipped out of her cubicle and was already standing at the sink, staring at her reflection in the unforgiving mirror, when Rachel Whitticker emerged from the other cubicle. The vomiting woman in the remaining stall stayed where she was. Rachel Whitticker washed her hands, careful not to look at either Ingrid or her reflection. Ingrid busied herself reapplying her lipstick.

After a long few moments of hand drying, the girl finally looked up and stared into Ingrid's eyes, via the mirror. "Is that particular shade of lipstick popular with the secret service this season?"

TWENTY-ONE

Ingrid decided to play dumb as a first line of defense. She would have felt more comfortable if the vomiting woman had left the bathroom. "I'm sorry, I don't understand," she said innocently.

"I knew you weren't an English cop, I just knew it!" There was a definite trill of excitement in Whitticker's tone: obviously thoroughly pleased with herself to have spotted an employee of the US government. "So, how long have you been working in the Diplomatic Security Service? This your first posting? I'm guessing not. Not many officers get a plum London job straight out the gate. Where were you before? Bratislava? Zagreb?"

Ingrid smiled at her indulgently. "I really do think you're mistaking me for somebody else."

"How the hell did you find me so fast?"

Ingrid merely shrugged at her.

"Look, I'm having a really nice time with my boyfriend. Can't you at least let me stay until dessert? I swear I was going back to Paris tonight. My grandmother need never even know I was gone."

The woman in the cubicle retched again.

"You OK in there?" Rachel asked. "Want me to get some help?"

"It's all right," came the feeble reply, "better out than in."

Rachel shuffled closer to Ingrid, she dropped her voice to a whisper. "Please don't get me in trouble with Grandma. She'll be so pissed at me. I've betrayed her trust. I don't know how much research you've done, but believe it or not, that's never actually happened before."

Ingrid decided to dispense with her unconvincing innocent act. "Maybe you should have thought about that before you embarked on your little adventure."

"You *are* secret service."

"Not exactly."

"Diplomatic Security? Please tell me Grandma doesn't know already."

"FBI." Ingrid shouldn't have told her. But her instinctive loyalty to the Bureau kicked in before she could do anything about it.

"Does that mean she *doesn't* know?"

"You need to come with me now, to the embassy."

"No way. I'll go back to Paris, I promise. Just as soon as the ball is over. Come on—let me spend a little more time with Eugene. I've come all this way, after all."

"That can't happen. Everything's arranged."

"OK—you win, I'm busted. But at least let me say goodbye to him."

"You can call him just as soon as we arrive at the embassy."

The woman in the cubicle retched again, more violently this time, and Ingrid glanced toward the toilet door. The moment her attention was distracted, the girl ducked around her and scooted toward the restroom door. She yanked it open, but Ingrid was on her before she'd managed to take a step outside. She laid a restraining hand on her upper arm.

"Nice try. But like you said, you're busted."

"But I have it all under control. A few hours here, back on the Eurostar to Paris, and my grandmother need never know I went away. Please… where's the harm in a little white lie?"

"I have my orders." If Rachel Whitticker really thought she stood a chance of persuading Ingrid to let her go, she was less smart than they'd all supposed.

"Now you just sound like the rest of them. Have a heart."

Ingrid squeezed the girl's arm a little tighter.

"Ow! You're hurting me!"

Shouts and yells sounded from the other end of the corridor. Ingrid peered outside from her position, half in, half out the restroom, to see a gang of what she supposed were highly privileged young Conservatives heading toward them. Their ties were askew and their shirts were stained with red wine. For some reason they'd decided to visit the men's restroom en masse.

Ingrid tugged on Rachel Whitticker's arm. Better to get her safely back into the ladies' until the drunken gang had passed by. The girl pulled against her. Ingrid tugged on her arm again.

Then she took a deep breath and screamed at the top of her lungs.

"Help me!" she cried, directing her plea toward the gang of drunken men. "This woman's trying to steal my purse."

Immediately the group of young men reared up as one, stared from Rachel Whitticker to Ingrid, couldn't quite process what was going on, then looked helplessly at one another.

"I'm really scared she's going to hurt me," Rachel Whitticker whined. "Help me."

All eyes then trained on Ingrid. This was not what she needed.

"Hey, move along guys. I'm an FBI agent."

"Oh yeah, sure… of course you bloody are. Get your filthy thieving hands off her," the tallest and widest of the group threatened. He looked her up and down. "How the hell did you get in here anyway?"

Ingrid glanced at her tiny purse, preparing to grab her ID, when she realized that she had jettisoned her badge in favor of her cell phone, some cash and a credit card. At the same time she must have unconsciously loosened her grip on the girl's shoulder, because a moment later Rachel Whitticker shrugged away from her and ran into the crowd of drunken, and now mildly angry, men and weaved her way through. Ingrid tried to follow, but the men closed in around her.

Holy crap.

"Hey—let me pass." Through the gaps between their heads she saw Rachel had almost reached the end of the corridor. "I mean it! Get the hell out of my way!"

The crush of bodies squeezed tighter. But not tight enough.

Ingrid had space enough to pull back her elbow and jab the guy nearest to her in the throat. As he staggered back, she kneed the guy next to him in the groin, and quickly brought a spear-like stiletto down as hard as she could into the next man's ankle. The other men blocking her path threw up their hands and quickly pressed themselves against the wall to allow her to pass.

Ingrid ran as fast as she could down the corridor, but the narrowness of her dress and the height of her heels made it almost impossible to pick up any speed. She stopped, kicked off the shoes and tore long rips into the sides of the dress. She picked up the shoes—they were too good a weapon to discard—and sprinted down the corridor. At the end she bundled through the door.

There was no sign of Rachel Whitticker on the other side. But there was a hell of a lot of noise. Banging and crashing and hollering. Swiftly followed by the shattering of glass. Twenty yards ahead of her, a man stumbled through a set of swing doors, struggling hard to stay on his feet, a tray of entrées held high above his head.

Ingrid ran toward him, then burst through the swing doors into a steamy, cramped kitchen. Through the clouds of steam she saw Rachel Whitticker's red dress disappear through another door. She started to follow, but a meaty, hairy arm blocked her path.

"FBI! Let me pass!"

The arm belonged to a six foot tall, two-hundred and fifty pound man, who was looking down at her stockinged feet. "There's broken glass all over this floor," he told her.

Goddammit.

Just as Ingrid started to force her feet back into the silver stilettos, she was lifted clean off the ground, carried across the kitchen, and deposited at the rear exit on the far side.

"Thank you," she hollered over her shoulder as she scrambled up a flight of concrete steps leading to the street.

She stood on the sidewalk and glanced right. From her sketchy knowledge of London, she was pretty sure she was looking in the direction of Trafalgar Square. In the distance to her left were the Houses of Parliament. There was no sign of Rachel Whitticker in either direction. Ingrid thumped a fist against her thigh. How could she have been so lax? She should never have allowed the girl to reach the door of the ladies' room. It was her job to bring her in and she had screwed it up.

She couldn't let the whole mission fail just because of a stupid rookie mistake.

TWENTY-TWO

Again Ingrid glanced toward the Houses of Parliament. She stared hard, hoping to make out movement of a bright red object in the distance. Mercifully, a second or so later, she was rewarded with exactly that.

Sixty yards up the street she caught a glimpse of Rachel Whitticker disappearing into a black taxi. The cab turned one-eighty degrees and started heading in Ingrid's direction, north toward Trafalgar Square. The taxi picked up speed.

Ingrid stepped into the street. Directly into its path.

She saw the driver's eyes widen to form big white circles as he stared straight at her. She stuck out both her arms. The driver tried swerving to his left to avoid her, but the inside lane was blocked by a slow moving pedal-powered rickshaw.

The driver's mouth fell open.

Only a dozen or so yards from Ingrid, he stamped on his brake. She saw him close his eyes. The tires screeched along the blacktop as the cab hurtled toward her. There just wasn't enough space for it to stop in time.

Ingrid sprang upwards and sideways, launching herself toward the sidewalk. She landed awkwardly in a half-somersault and rolled over. She gasped for air, gulping down shallow breaths as she tried to right herself into a crouch.

One of the taxi's rear doors swung open.

Rachel Whitticker jumped out and started to run. Ingrid watched as the girl pumped her arms, her long legs pounding up and down like pistons. She was running north up the center of the street, toward Trafalgar Square.

Ingrid struggled to her feet. She searched desperately for her purse, finally locating it next to the curb, balancing on a storm drain. Its contents had spilled out. She quickly scooped up the cash and the cell phone and started to run after the escaping girl. Discovering the sidewalk was too busy, she too ran toward the central reservation. The blacktop felt hard and sharp beneath her feet, pain pressing into her bare soles with every step, hampering her movement. Rachel Whitticker was wearing a sensible pair of ballet pumps. The road surface didn't seem to be bothering her one little bit.

Way into the distance, Ingrid could see the sidewalk on both sides of the street was full of tourists and holiday revelers making their way to the square. She had to get to Rachel before the girl merged with the crowd. Ingrid gulped down more air and accelerated. She didn't even notice the big red bus until it blasted its horn at her as she scooted across a right hand turn. She missed getting hit by inches and only lost a little of her forward momentum. She glanced up. The girl was just fifty or so yards from the edge of Trafalgar Square. Ingrid forced every last ounce of energy from her tiring muscles.

After a few moments she got the sense she was gaining on her prey a little. She tried to pump her arms faster, but there was no more left in them. Up ahead, she noticed Rachel had stopped, forced to wait for a gap in the traffic to reach the square itself. Every few seconds she glanced toward Ingrid, then from side to side, maybe looking for another escape route. But wherever she looked, the flow of vehicles was relentless. Ingrid knew that pretty soon the lights would change and the girl would be able to sprint into the masses roaming across the square and disappear completely.

But Ingrid still had momentum on her side. She carried on, despite the screaming protests of the muscles in her arms and legs. She was forty yards from the crossing. Thirty. Twenty. Just ten yards out, the signal changed and Rachel started to run. Ingrid had almost closed the distance between them.

Just fifteen feet behind, Ingrid reached out an arm, but the motion slowed her down. The girl remained tantalizingly out of reach. As Ingrid flew across the road she let out a howl of frustration. She should never have let the situation come to this. If she lost her now…

Rachel Whitticker reached the wide, gray-slabbed pavement on the other side of the crossing and then headed toward the big tall column on the south side of the square. She ducked to the right and ran around one of the four massive lion sculptures.

Out of sight.

Ingrid traced her steps and spotted her again just beyond another of the lions.

Rachel started hollering at the tourists to get out of her way, clearing a path for herself, but also leaving a channel clear for Ingrid to follow in her wake. The girl ran between the two ornate fountains and reached a giant Christmas tree decorated with hundreds of white lights. A moment later she changed direction, and started heading east. Ingrid gained another second. She could be no more than ten feet away. Again she stretched out a hand.

This time she made contact with Rachel Whitticker's long hair. She grabbed a fistful and yanked. The girl stopped dead. Ingrid careened right into her and knocked them both to the ground. Ingrid quickly swiveled around, planted one foot either side of the girl's legs and sat heavily on her butt.

Rachel Whitticker screamed and wriggled wildly beneath her. A couple of passers-by had stopped and were staring at them. "One glass of champagne too many," Ingrid said by way of explanation. The two tourists looked at her blankly. Then started taking photographs. Ingrid shook her head in disbelief and held up a hand to obscure her face. When the tourists finally lost interest and wandered away, she loosened her grip on the cell phone she been clutching and quickly found Angelis' number. The call rang out three, four times.

Come on!

He picked up on the fifth.

"Where the hell are you?" he barked at her.

More tourists had started to gather to see the spectacle of two women in evening dresses writhing beneath a giant Christmas tree.

"Trafalgar Square. I need a car here. Fast."

TWENTY-THREE

The next day Ingrid's presence was requested at the embassy by the deputy chief of mission, Sol Franklin's boss. At the time, the phone call had seemed not so much a request as an outright demand. Ingrid had no choice but to comply.

When she arrived at four p.m., she was greeted at reception by two Diplomatic Security agents: a man and a woman both dressed in regulation black suits and white shirts. They escorted her, in silence, to the fifth floor. She was led into a room very similar to the one she and Lucille had been left in just the day before. This time, however, no one had demanded she give them her cell phone and the door remained unlocked. She settled back on one of the couches and, with nothing more meaningful to do, took the opportunity to delete all the old emails from her phone. As she first scanned, then deleted the old emails, she let her mind drift.

The last twenty-four hours had been the most exciting she'd experienced in years. For her, that kind of adrenalin rush was impossible to achieve any other way. She had been entrusted by a superior officer with a time critical and highly classified task. Despite the odds being stacked against her, she'd delivered. As far as Ingrid was concerned, the sense of satisfaction that came with the successful conclusion of a mission just couldn't be matched.

The night before, Rachel Whitticker had been whisked away in a black limousine, not to the embassy, as expected, but to an unknown location, leaving Ingrid to catch a ride from Trafalgar Square with Angelis. As soon as she'd settled herself into the back of the embassy sedan, she'd asked him about the change of plan.

"They're taking her straight to Paris," he'd told her. "Skipping the London day trip cover story entirely. It turns out the peace talks will be continuing until well after midnight. If the Secretary of State wants to contact her granddaughter when she eventually emerges, we're going to make sure young Rachel is tucked up safe and sound in her hotel room, ready to take that call."

"Will the talks be resuming tomorrow morning?" Ingrid asked.

"That's the scheduled final session. When everyone hopes a breakthrough will happen. Thanks to your efforts, that'll be the only thing Secretary of State Whitticker will have to think about."

"What has Barclay been told? Does he even know Rachel's true identity?"

"Doesn't seem that way. Maybe he'll never find out."

"He will if Rachel follows through with her plan to piss off her parents."

"Not our concern, this round of negotiations will be over by then. Nothing Rachel does from now on will be able to jeopardize them."

Ingrid let out a long sigh.

"Does it seem rather an anti-climax?"

"Not at all, I'm glad we pulled it off."

"Less of the modesty. You pretty much resolved the situation on your own." He smiled at her. "Bloody well done you." He lifted his hand toward her right knee, let it hover there for a moment, then withdrew it. "I'd say a celebration is in order."

"I'm exhausted."

"I insist. A little late supper and a nightcap."

Credit to Angelis—he'd behaved impeccably. After supper he'd escorted her to her hotel room, the only sign of his previous flirtatiousness a gentle peck on the back of her hand.

There was a sharp knock on the door. Ingrid jumped slightly, brought back from her memories of the night before with a bump. She shoved her phone into a pocket and stood up. "Come in."

The door opened. "They're ready for you now," the Marine standing in the doorway told her.

"They?"

"Would you follow me, please?"

Ingrid did exactly as she was told and followed the Marine to the elevator. They traveled one floor up to the sixth. He led her along a rosewood paneled corridor and into a very grand room at the far end. Waiting for her inside were Sol Franklin and Nick Angelis. She greeted them both with a formal handshake and spent a moment taking in the surroundings. There was plush cream carpet covering the floor, an enormous desk opposite the door with two silk upholstered chairs on the right hand side. The American flag was proudly attached to the wall behind the desk.

"Is this the ambassador's office?" Ingrid asked Sol.

"It is."

"Am I going to meet her?"

"Actually Ambassador Byrne-Williams is out of the country until later this evening."

"Oh." Ingrid glanced around the room again. "So what am I doing here?"

"There's someone else I'd like you to meet."

A moment later, almost as if he'd planned it that way, the door opened and a half dozen security agents entered the room. In their wake was Rachel Whitticker, who gave Ingrid a subtle wave. Behind her was a tall, red haired woman wearing a regulation dark suit and bright white shirt. She didn't look secret service. The cut of her jacket seemed far too expensive for someone on a government pay grade.

"One of Fortnum's finest," Angelis murmured in Ingrid's ear. "She won't let Rachel out of her sight."

The agents took up positions at the corners of the room and either side of the large desk.

Ingrid stared expectantly at the doorway. Just a second later a woman dressed in a navy blue wool Chanel suit glided into the room. Sol Franklin hurried to greet her.

"Madam Secretary," he said, and guided her toward Angelis and Ingrid.

"It appears I owe you a great debt," the Secretary of State said.

Ingrid glanced first at Sol, then at Rachel Whitticker. "Ma'am?"

"Oh, it's all right. No need for secrecy now. I found out all about Rachel's little adventure earlier this afternoon. My daughter-in-law informed me." She gave her granddaughter a stern look. "I also know exactly what you did to save the day."

Sol was beaming and nodding enthusiastically at Ingrid like a proud dad.

"I was just doing what was requested of me."

"It's hardly the way you expected to spend your time in London."

"No, ma'am, it certainly wasn't."

"I'm glad you were around. I hope you don't mind being summoned here like this. When I found out what had happened, I wanted to thank you personally." She held Ingrid's right hand in both of hers. "I appreciate everything you've done."

Ingrid was painfully aware just how moist her palm was. She wanted to apologize for it, but decided it was better to say nothing. She'd never met anyone she admired quite as much as Jayne Whitticker before. The woman had fought for equality in the sixties and seventies, been a leading light at the United Nations in the nineties, and was now brokering peace in a war torn region of Africa. Ingrid was just grateful her hand hadn't started to tremble as well.

"Given what she put you through, you might be interested to hear Rachel has been grounded for the next month." Although the Secretary of State was glaring at her granddaughter, a faint smile played around her lips.

Ingrid wondered exactly how long the grounding would be enforced.

Jayne Whitticker shook Angelis' hand and swiftly turned on her heels. Ingrid watched her glide back out the room, followed by her granddaughter, her granddaughter's bodyguard, the Diplomatic Security agents and Nick Angelis. A few moments later Ingrid was standing alone in the ambassador's office with Sol Franklin.

"She really did want to thank you personally. It was her idea. Took a little organizing, I've got to admit. But we got there in the end, huh?"

"It was worth every second." Ingrid blew out a breath.

"So, how was your introduction to the Legal Attaché program?"

"Quite a roller coaster ride."

"I'd be lying if I told you it was quite that exciting around here all the time. But we have our moments."

Ingrid's work at the VCAC had been a little like treading water in recent months. She hadn't felt a sense of achievement for some time.

"How'd you like the idea of maybe taking on another case?"

"I don't understand."

"We have a vacancy here in the criminal division. You seem like the ideal candidate for the job."

Ingrid blinked. She had been standing there anticipating a little speech from Sol Franklin about the need for absolute discretion regarding Rachel Whitticker's European adventure, not a job offer.

"I've discussed it with the chief of mission. He'd need to meet you before any final decision is made. But I've been singing your praises so loud, his approval would pretty much be a formality."

"I… I… ah…" Ingrid really didn't know how to respond.

"Your plane doesn't leave till this evening. You've got a little time to consider it."

Ingrid thought about what was waiting for her when she got home: a cold apartment, an empty refrigerator and a fiancé who she hardly ever saw. But she couldn't leave her post at the Violent Crimes Against Children program at such short notice.

"Thank you for the offer, I really appreciate it. But—"

"Don't turn me down flat. Take some time to really give it some thought. Talk it over with your fiancé."

The thought of discussing an overseas posting with Marshall wasn't one she relished. He'd already been putting pressure on her to pick a date for the wedding.

Sol Franklin must have seen the internal conflict flicker across her face. He said, "You could even take on the job on a short term, temporary basis. Three to six months, maybe, see how you like it." He really did seem eager to have her work there.

"OK—I won't turn you down now."

Sol grinned at her. "Good! Great!"

"But I'm not making any promises."

"Why not take a little time out this afternoon? See the sights. Do a little shopping. Let the idea percolate at the back of your mind." He started to move toward the door. "We should get out of here. The ambassador's secretary might get a little pissed otherwise."

He escorted her all the way to reception. "I know you'll make the right decision." With that he waved her goodbye.

Ingrid wandered toward Grosvenor Square in a daze. She'd just been offered a dream job and hadn't jumped at the opportunity. What was wrong with her? A tall figure stepped in front of her. She blinked and looked up into the smiling face of Nick Angelis.

"What the hell are you doing here?" she asked him, all thoughts of the job offer quickly banished from her mind.

"How did you enjoy your little surprise? It's not every day you get to meet the Secretary of State."

"She's a very gracious woman." Ingrid wasn't sure when her heart rate would return to normal, but she wasn't about to admit that to Angelis.

"She certainly is. I think she'll be a formidable Secretary of State. The peace talks went better than anyone expected. She's back in a couple of weeks for another round of negotiations. Without her granddaughter next time, one would hope."

"Good for her."

"And what about you?"

"What about me?"

"Your job offer."

"You know about that?"

"I am in the intelligence business." He winked at her.

"I told Sol I'd think about it. But I suppose you know that already too."

Angelis smiled and gestured toward his motorcycle parked across the street. "Your carriage awaits."

"My what?" Despite her better judgment, she found herself following him to the bike.

"You deserve a proper guided tour of this fair city, and by God, that's exactly what you're going to get." They reached the bike and he handed her a motorcycle helmet. "I'll let London itself influence your decision to stay. I have to warn you—it'll be quite a compelling case."

Ingrid shoved the helmet over her head and climbed on the bike. Maybe a few months away from home, from the VCAC program, and a little distance from Marshall, might help her decide what she actually wanted to do with her life. She felt herself warming slightly to the idea of a few months in another country.

And maybe a little adventure of her own.

By the time Angelis had ridden them past the major landmarks of central London, with a running commentary of the history of each one, bought her coffee in two of the finest coffee shops she'd ever visited, and shown her the cityscape in its full glory from Primrose Hill, a spectacular vantage point just north of London Zoo, Ingrid was completely sold on the idea.

For a little while at least, London was going to be home.

THE ADVENTURES OF INGRID SKYBERG CONTINUE IN THE BESTSELLING NOVEL, **FRESH DOUBT**

TURN THE PAGE FOR A SNEAK PREVIEW

FRESH DOUBT

An Ingrid Skyberg FBI Thriller

Eva Hudson

ONE

The whole thing took less than a few seconds. A moment to shove the woman sideways, another to drag the straps of the purse from her shoulder, then finally a second more to snatch and scoop the bag into his arms. Then the young Caucasian male was away, barging into a crowd of early morning office workers making their way sedately along the Thames just east of Waterloo railway station.

Special Agent Ingrid Skyberg saw it all happen in slow-mo as she ran past. She glimpsed the woman's mouth form a wide silent 'O', throw up her hands in disbelief then scream at the top of her lungs.

Ingrid had just been getting into her stride, feeling her muscles warm, absorbing the faint heat of the early morning April sun on her face.

"Goddammit," she said to no one in particular, "why this morning?"

She pulled up fast—the perp was escaping behind her—and turned on a dime. A few seconds later she was in pursuit, all her previous momentum moving with her again as she tried to accelerate through the crowd.

"Stop!" she shouted, pumping her arms faster. "FBI!" Then she remembered herself, threw a glance over her shoulder and yelled at the mugging victim to call 9-1-1. The woman looked at Ingrid blankly. "I mean 9-9-9, call 9-9-9!"

Ingrid turned face front again and quickly realized she'd lost the perp. She scanned a sea of mildly disgruntled faces and shouted at them to get the hell out of her way. Scrutinizing the very edges of the crowd, she spotted him again, his shaven bright white head appearing a few inches above the general mass of commuters. She formalized his description in her head for later. White, male, five-eleven, one-seventy pounds, bald head, no more than twenty years of age. For a moment she considered grabbing her phone to relay the details to the local cops when the cell started to vibrate, tingling against her bicep. Whoever it was would have to wait.

The crowd cleaved in two in front of her, opening a central channel. Ingrid pumped her arms harder and gulped a deep breath, forcing air into her lungs as they were just starting to burn. She lengthened her stride and lifted her chin a little. She was starting to enjoy herself. She hadn't felt this alert since the last Academy refresher course. And that had to be at least six months ago. No, longer. She quickly counted the weeks she'd been in the UK and realized she hadn't been home for over four months. The embassy job was meant to be a temporary posting. How had she let it stretch out this long?

Thirty yards ahead of her the perp changed direction, darting quickly right, away from the river, and up a spiral flight of bright yellow painted concrete steps. He was tiring and Ingrid was gaining on him with every stride. "Stop! Police!" she yelled, as she took the first four steps in a single leap. She pushed hard against the concrete spiral with her arms, using the extra momentum as leverage to shoot her up the staircase faster. She looked up just in time to see a bottle of water hurtling toward her from above. She ducked quickly left, the half liter of Evian bouncing harmlessly off her shoulder.

"Sonofa…"

When she reached the top of the steps she located her quarry crossing an expanse of concrete paving, discarding items from the woman's purse as he went. Finally he dropped the bag itself, but held on to a bright pink pocket book. He ran toward a set of steps leading down to the road at the back of the Royal Festival Hall. She couldn't let him reach the road. There were too many escape routes at street level.

She lengthened her stride, for a split second enjoying the lactic burn in her quads. He was only a dozen or so yards ahead now. Three yards out she lurched forward and snatched at his jacket, managing to catch the hem in a fist. The sudden jerking movement forced the pink wallet from his hand and it flew into the air. Ingrid pulled up sharp and yanked hard on his jacket, then attempted to reel him in. When his head was only inches from hers, her cell phone started buzzing again. She couldn't ignore it again. Distracted for a moment, she didn't see the perp wriggle free of the constrains of his coat until he had slipped right out of her hands.

He glanced at her, eyed the pocketbook on the ground, hesitated a moment longer, then flung himself toward the metal stairway. When he reached it he stopped, turned and gave Ingrid the finger before running down the steps.

Ingrid had to resist the temptation to follow him. Right now she had more important things to attend to. She snatched the cell phone from its pouch. "Agent Skyberg."

"You took your time."

"I've been making the streets safer for the good citizens of London."

Almost.

She stooped down and snatched the wallet from the ground and then retraced her steps, gathering items as she went, a treasure trail of the content of every woman's purse. She pulled up short at the packet of condoms. Ingrid supposed it was always best to be prepared. Even at eight a.m. on a Monday morning. "What's up, Sol?" She wondered briefly why the assistant to the deputy section chief was calling her himself.

Sol cleared his throat. Then started to cough. Ingrid had to pull the phone from her ear while she waited for him to compose himself. Finally there was silence at the other end. Either the assistant deputy had choked to death or he was quietly wiping the tears from his eyes.

"Sol?"

She heard a deep inhale. "Deputy Chief Louden has personally requested you deal with this case urgently."

Louden?

"Get yourself down to St Pancras Hotel—in King's Cross. The… ah… victim is waiting for you there."

TWO

Sol proceeded to give Ingrid the lowdown on her new assignment as she jogged back to the mugging victim with the woman's purse. Sol had resolutely refused to tell Ingrid why the deputy chief had taken such an interest in this new assignment, despite her asking him more than once. He simply told her he would text the address to her and hung up.

Two uniformed cops, one male, one female, both on bicycles, were talking to the woman who'd had her purse snatched, one had a pen poised over his notebook. Ingrid handed the woman back her belongings. She managed to find a dog-eared business card in her pocket and handed it to the female cop. "I don't have time to give you a statement right now," Ingrid explained. "Call me this afternoon."

The police officer peered down at the rectangle of embossed card. "FBI? Is this a joke?"

"Call the US embassy after lunch—they'll patch you through to me."

The cop looked up and down the river path, searching for something. "Where are the cameras?"

"What?" Ingrid really didn't have time for this right now.

"You're filming something, right?" The cop nudged her colleague whose mouth had dropped open.

"You're that… erm… that actress… the one who—"

"No." Ingrid took off her baseball cap. "I'm not." She forced a smile. "Just be sure and call me this afternoon if you need another description of the perp." She tucked her short hair back under her cap.

The mugging victim was staring at her intensely now too. "I can see it myself. You do look a bit like her. Except for the short hair, of course. What's her name? Charlize… thingummy. Anyway…" She reached into her wallet. "Thanks ever so much for getting my bag back. I'd be lost without my phone. Here…" She waved a crisp twenty pound note at Ingrid. "Take something for your trouble."

Ingrid held up both hands, resisted the temptation to say "just doing my job, ma'am" and sprinted back to where she'd parked her motorcycle.

She reached her hotel in Marylebone in less than ten minutes. The Triumph Tiger 800 wasn't a Harley, but it handled pretty well, especially weaving through rush hour traffic in central London. She parked up in the underground parking lot and took the emergency stairs to the fourth floor. Ten feet from her room she pulled up. The door was open six or so inches. She checked the hallway left and right—no sign of the linen cart. She pictured her FBI issue Glock 23 nestling in its locked metal case within the safe inside the closet. There were at least thirty seconds between

Ingrid and the gun. More than enough time for an intruder to take her out and do whatever else it was they'd come here for. She pressed her back against the hallway wall and drew in a deep breath.

And listened.

Silence for a few seconds then a noisy metallic clang sounded from inside the room. Ingrid pushed open the door a few more inches and peered through the gap. There was no one in the bedroom. A second later she heard a high-pitched scream. It was coming from the bathroom. Ingrid rushed toward the sound, yanking the bedside table lamp from its socket on her way to the bathroom. The scream modulated suddenly into a yodel.

What the…?

Ingrid stopped just short of the bathroom door. Inside she saw a chambermaid wearing a huge pair of headphones. The woman was bending over the toilet, scrubbing the inside of the pan in time to the tinny beat issuing from the headphones. Grabbing her lower back, the woman straightened up and turned toward Ingrid. Ingrid quickly shoved the lamp behind her back and plastered on a smile. The maid froze when she saw her and clutched a thick-fingered hand to her chest, then smiled broadly, her mouth busy with Eastern European metal dental-ware. She said something in Russian, the thick accent placing her country of origin somewhere on the northeastern side of the Black Sea. Although Ingrid was tempted to respond to the woman in her native tongue, she just smiled sweetly and backed out of the room as the maid awkwardly rotated her cleaning cart one-eighty degrees and dragged it from the cramped bathroom.

The maid was new. The regular maid, a much younger woman, always left the cart in the hallway outside. Ingrid shooed this maid out of the room, returning her extravagant nods and smiles in kind. “Come back later,” she said firmly and slammed the door.

After checking her handgun was still stored securely in the safe, Ingrid showered and dressed quickly, choosing a somber dark gray pant suit from her small collection of work clothes. Yet again she made a mental note to visit a Banana Republic to purchase one or two alternative suits when she next had the chance. When she’d packed for her five-day London trip, she’d had no clue she would still be living out of a suitcase four months later. But then she hadn’t expected to be offered a job in the US embassy criminal division. As she dabbed a smudge of mascara under her left eye she promised herself she’d do something to fix her wardrobe and her living arrangements. Sometime. Soon.

Already running perilously late, she chose to forego her usual wheatgrass juice in the coffee shop next to the hotel and went straight for her regular double espresso chaser. Fifteen minutes later she was climbing off her motorcycle in the forecourt of the St Pancras Hotel in King’s Cross. Her cell started to buzz. She grabbed it from her bag, saw it was an “out of area” number and hit the “dismiss” option. It was very probably her fiancé calling to boast about a successful conclusion to his latest investigation. Or maybe he wanted to tell her about yet another new promotion.

Marshall and his ever-growing ego could wait.

She shoved the phone back in her bag, hurried through the main entrance and headed straight for the elevator and the fifth floor.

Sol had given her only sketchy details of the assignment. She had a name, a room number and basic outline of the crime. She still hadn't managed to work out why the deputy chief had taken such an interest in the case. Perhaps the victim himself would be able to enlighten her. Usually a simple robbery would have been reported to the local cops, with Ingrid, or more likely one of the civilian members of the embassy staff, liaising with them afterward. But it seemed Greg Brewster was far too important to be left to deal with the situation without higher-level US embassy representation.

She quickly found the room on the fifth floor and knocked twice, good and hard. The door opened three inches, restrained by a metal safety catch.

"Where the hell have you been?"

ALSO BY EVA HUDSON

Ingrid Skyberg FBI Thrillers

Fresh Doubt
Kill Plan
Deep Hurt
The Skyberg Files

Angela Tate Investigations

The Loyal Servant
The Deadly Silence

and

The Senior Moment

Available now in paperback and ebook

About the author

Eva was born and raised in London. She's been a local government worker, web editor, dotcom entrepreneur, portrait artist and singer. She wrote her first novel in 2005 and has never looked back.

In 2011 Eva won the inaugural Lucy Cavendish Prize for Fiction for her first published novel, *The Loyal Servant.* The book was also shortlisted for TV's People's Novelist Award.

Eva lives in Sussex and London, and loves to spend time in the US.

You can catch up with news about Eva on her website, evahudson.com, and follow her on Twitter (twitter.com/Eva_Hudson) and on Facebook (facebook.com/evahudsoncrimewriter).

RUN GIRL

EVA HUDSON

– VENATRIX –

11842602R00103

Printed in Great Britain
by Amazon.co.uk, Ltd.,
Marston Gate.